BASIL THOMSON
THE CASE OF THE DEAD DIPLOMAT

Sir Basil Home Thomson (1861-1939) was educated at Eton and New College Oxford. After spending a year farming in Iowa, he married in 1889 and worked for the Foreign Service. This included a stint working alongside the Prime Minister of Tonga (according to some accounts, he *was* the Prime Minister of Tonga) in the 1890s followed by a return to the Civil Service and a period as Governor of Dartmoor Prison. He was Assistant Commissioner to the Metropolitan Police from 1913 to 1919, after which he moved into Intelligence. He was knighted in 1919 and received other honours from Europe and Japan, but his public career came to an end when he was arrested for committing an act of indecency in Hyde Park in 1925 – an incident much debated and disputed.

His eight crime novels featuring series character Inspector Richardson were written in the 1930's and received great praise from Dorothy L. Sayers among others. He also wrote biographical and criminological works.

Also by Basil Thomson

Richardson's First Case
Richardson Scores Again
The Case of Naomi Clynes
The Dartmoor Enigma
Who Killed Stella Pomeroy?
The Milliner's Hat Mystery
A Murder is Arranged

BASIL THOMSON

THE CASE OF
THE DEAD DIPLOMAT

With an introduction by
Martin Edwards

DEAN STREET PRESS

Published by Dean Street Press 2016

First published in 1935 by Eldon Press as
Richardson Goes Abroad

Cover by DSP

Introduction © Martin Edwards 2016

ISBN 978 1 911095 73 6

www.deanstreetpress.co.uk

Introduction

Sir Basil Thomson's stranger-than-fiction life was packed so full of incident that one can understand why his work as a crime novelist has been rather overlooked. This was a man whose CV included spells as a colonial administrator, prison governor, intelligence officer, and Assistant Commissioner at Scotland Yard. Among much else, he worked alongside the Prime Minister of Tonga (according to some accounts, he *was* the Prime Minister of Tonga), interrogated Mata Hari and Roger Casement (although not at the same time), and was sensationally convicted of an offence of indecency committed in Hyde Park. More than three-quarters of a century after his death, he deserves to be recognised for the contribution he made to developing the police procedural, a form of detective fiction that has enjoyed lasting popularity.

Basil Home Thomson was born in 1861 – the following year his father became Archbishop of York – and was educated at Eton before going up to New College. He left Oxford after a couple of terms, apparently as a result of suffering depression, and joined the Colonial Service. Assigned to Fiji, he became a stipendiary magistrate before moving to Tonga. Returning to England in 1893, he published *South Sea Yarns*, which is among the 22 books written by him which are listed in Allen J. Hubin's comprehensive bibliography of crime fiction (although in some cases, the criminous content was limited).

Thomson was called to the Bar, but opted to become deputy governor of Liverpool Prison; he later served as governor of such prisons as Dartmoor and Wormwood Scrubs, and acted as secretary to the Prison Commission. In 1913, he became head of C.I.D., which acted as the enforcement arm of British military intelligence after war broke out. When the Dutch exotic dancer and alleged spy Mata Hari arrived in England in 1916, she was arrested and interviewed at length by Thomson at Scotland Yard; she was released, only to be shot the following year by a French firing squad. He gave an account of the interrogation in *Queer People* (1922).

Thomson was knighted, and given the additional responsibility of acting as Director of Intelligence at the Home Office, but in 1921, he was controversially ousted, prompting a heated debate in Parliament: according to *The Times*, "for a few minutes there was pandemonium". The government argued that Thomson was at odds with the Commissioner of the Metropolitan Police, Sir William Horwood (whose own career ended with an ignominious departure fromoffice seven years later), but it seems likely be that covert political machinations lay behind his removal. With many aspects of Thomson's complex life, it is hard to disentangle fiction from fact.

Undaunted, Thomson resumed his writing career, and in 1925, he published *Mr Pepper Investigates*, a collection of humorous short mysteries, the most renowned of which is "The Vanishing of Mrs Fraser". In the same year, he was arrested in Hyde Park for "committing an act in violation of public decency" with a young woman who gave her name as Thelma de Lava. Thomson protested his innocence, but in vain: his trial took place amid a blaze of publicity, and he was fined five pounds. Despite the fact that Thelma de Lava had pleaded guilty (her fine was reportedly paid by a photographer), Thomson launched an appeal, claiming that he was the victim of a conspiracy, but the court would have none of it. Was he framed, or the victim of entrapment? If so, was the reason connected with his past work in intelligence or crime solving? The answers remain uncertain, but Thomson's equivocal responses to the police after being apprehended damaged his credibility.

Public humiliation of this kind would have broken a less formidable man, but Thomson, by now in his mid-sixties, proved astonishingly resilient. A couple of years after his trial, he was appointed to reorganise the Siamese police force, and he continued to produce novels. These included *The Kidnapper* (1933), which Dorothy L. Sayers described in a review for the *Sunday Times* as "not so much a detective story as a sprightly fantasia upon a detective theme." She approved the fact that Thomson wrote "good English very amusingly", and noted that "some of his characters have real charm." Mr Pepper returned in *The Kidnapper*, but in the same year, Thomson introduced his most important character, a Scottish policeman called Richardson.

Thomson took advantage of his inside knowledge to portray a young detective climbing through the ranks at Scotland Yard. And Richardson's rise is amazingly rapid: thanks to the fastest fast-tracking imaginable, he starts out as a police constable, and has become Chief Constable by the time of his seventh appearance – in a book published only four years after the first. We learn little about Richardson's background beyond the fact that he comes of Scottish farming stock, but he is likeable as well as highly efficient, and his sixth case introduces him to his future wife. His inquiries take him – and other colleagues – not only to different parts of England but also across the Channel on more than one occasion: in *The Case of the Dead Diplomat*, all the action takes place in France. There is a zest about the stories, especially when compared with some of the crime novels being produced at around the same time, which is striking, especially given that all of them were written by a man in his seventies.

From the start of the series, Thomson takes care to show the team work necessitated by a criminal investigation. Richardson is a key connecting figure, but the importance of his colleagues' efforts is never minimised in order to highlight his brilliance. In *The Case of the Dead Diplomat*, for instance, it is the trusty

Sergeant Cooper who makes good use of his linguistic skills and flair for impersonation to trap the villains of the piece. Inspector Vincent takes centre stage in *The Milliner's Hat Mystery*, with Richardson confined to the background. He is more prominent in *A Murder is Arranged*, but it is Inspector Dallas who does most of the leg-work.

Such a focus on police team-working is very familiar to present day crime fiction fans, but it was something fresh in the Thirties. Yet Thomson was not the first man with personal experience of police life to write crime fiction: Frank Froest, a legendary detective, made a considerable splash with his first novel, *The Grell Mystery*, published in 1913. Froest, though, was a career cop, schooled in "the university of life" without the benefit of higher education, who sought literary input from a journalist, George Dilnot, whereas Basil Thomson was a fluent and experienced writer whose light, brisk style is ideally suited to detective fiction, with its emphasis on entertainment. Like so many other detective novelists, his interest in "true crime" is occasionally apparent in his fiction, but although *Who Killed Stella Pomeroy?* opens with a murder scenario faintly reminiscent of the legendary Wallace case of 1930, the storyline soon veers off in a quite different direction.

Even before Richardson arrived on the scene, two accomplished detective novelists had created successful police series. Freeman Wills Crofts devised elaborate crimes (often involving ingenious alibis) for Inspector French to solve, and his books highlight the patience and meticulous work of the skilled police investigator. Henry Wade wrote increasingly ambitious novels, often featuring the Oxford-educated Inspector Poole, and exploring the tensions between police colleagues as well as their shared values. Thomson's mysteries are less convoluted than Crofts', and less sophisticated than Wade's, but they make pleasant reading. This is, at least in part, thanks to little touches of detail that are unquestionably authentic – such as senior officers' dread of newspaper criticism, as in *The Dartmoor Enigma*. No other crime writer, after all, has ever had such wide-ranging personal experience of prison management, intelligence work, the hierarchies of Scotland Yard, let alone a desperate personal fight, under the unforgiving glare of the media spotlight, to prove his innocence of a criminal charge sure to stain, if not destroy, his reputation.

Ingenuity was the hallmark of many of the finest detective novels written during "the Golden Age of murder" between the wars, and intricacy of plotting – at least judged by the standards of Agatha Christie, Anthony Berkeley, and John Dickson Carr – was not Thomson's true speciality. That said, *The Milliner's Hat Mystery* is remarkable for having inspired Ian Fleming, while he was working in intelligence during the Second World War, after Thomson's death. In a memo to Rear Admiral John Godfrey, Fleming said: "The following suggestion is used in a book by Basil Thomson: a corpse dressed as an airman, with despatches in his pockets, could be dropped on the coast, supposedly from a parachute that has failed. I understand there is no difficulty in obtaining corpses at the Naval Hospital, but, of course, it would have to be a fresh one." This clever idea became the basis for "Operation Mincemeat", a plan to conceal the invasion of Italy from North Africa.

A further intriguing connection between Thomson and Fleming is that Thomson inscribed copies of at least two of the Richardson books to Kathleen Pettigrew, who was personal assistant to the Director of MI6, Stewart Menzies. She is widely regarded as the woman on whom Fleming based Miss Moneypenny, secretary to James Bond's boss M – the Moneypenny character was originally called "Petty" Petteval. Possibly it was through her that Fleming came across Thomson's book.

Thomson's writing was of sufficiently high calibre to prompt Dorothy L. Sayers to heap praise on Richardson's performance in his third case: "he puts in some of that excellent, sober, straightforward detective work which he so well knows how to do and follows the clue of a post-mark to the heart of a very plausible and proper mystery. I find him a most agreeable companion." The acerbic American critics Jacques Barzun and Wendell Hertig Taylor also had a soft spot for Richardson, saying in *A Catalogue of Crime* that his investigations amount to "early police routine minus the contrived bickering, stomach ulcers, and pub-crawling with which later writers have masked poverty of invention and the dullness of repetitive questioning".

Books in the Richardson series have been out of print and hard to find for decades, and their reappearance at affordable prices is as welcome as it is overdue. Now that Dean Street Press have republished all eight recorded entries in the Richardson case-book, twenty-first century readers are likely to find his company just as agreeable as Sayers did.

Martin Edwards

www.martinedwardsbooks.com

Chapter One

Eric Carruthers, the first secretary at the Paris Embassy, was entertaining his fellow Scotsman, Guy Dundas, the newly joined attaché, at luncheon at a café discovered by himself, in which the cooking and the wine were both beyond criticism.

"You'll find, I'm afraid, that officially this place is not exciting. Nothing ever happens here."

"All the better. I shall have a better chance of learning my job," answered the younger man, who was fresh from Oxford and felt that his foot was on a rung of the ladder up which he dreamed of climbing rapidly. "At any rate you seem to be a happy family here."

"Oh, we don't quarrel and that is always something." Carruthers looked at his watch. "We ought to be getting along to the Chancery. Though nothing ever happens we must keep to official hours and it's half-past two."

They took a taxi back to the Embassy; the messenger was waiting on the steps of the Chancery.

"His Excellency has been waiting for you, sir," he said to Carruthers. "He is in his room now with Mr. Stirling, if you would kindly go up."

"Asking for *me*?"

"Yes, sir. His Excellency seemed very anxious to see you—told me to keep at the door and be sure to let you know as soon as you came in."

"Very good, Chubb; I'll go at once."

Dundas made his way to the little room in the Chancery where he spent his working hours in what his stable-companion, Ned Gregory, the third secretary, irreverently termed "licking stamps," but which actually consisted in such responsible duties as decoding cipher telegrams and making up the diplomatic bags for the courier. Gregory was not at his table; his voice could be heard holding forth in the next room; the Chancery seemed to be in a flutter. Dundas wondered whether the monotony of which Carruthers had complained was about to be broken.

Eric Carruthers found his chief collapsed in a deep arm-chair in the stately room where he received official visitors and signed dispatches. The Minister Plenipotentiary, Richard Stirling, was with him. Both wore an air of deep depression.

"I hope you are feeling better this morning, sir," was Carruthers' greeting. He knew that his chief had been brooding over his health and that the Embassy doctor, Dr. Hoskyn, was attending him daily. "They told me downstairs that you wanted to see me."

"I did. I suppose that you have heard the news about Everett. You seem to be taking it very easily."

"About Everett, sir? Has he been letting himself go with the native journalists?"

"He's dead."

There was a pause. Carruthers was trying to take in this startling intelligence; the ambassador leaned forward in his chair.

"Everett dead! Why, I saw him in the Chancery yesterday afternoon. He looked perfectly fit then and seemed in the best of spirits. What did he die of?"

"Suicide or murder, the police say. All I know is that a police *commissaire* from the ninth *arrondissement* called here three-quarters of an hour ago and gave a rambling account of the discovery of Everett's body in his own flat with a knife wound in the throat. They did not know who he was until they found his Embassy card in his pocket-book, and they then came down here to make inquiries."

"Who saw the *commissaire*, sir?"

"Maynard saw him and came upstairs to tell me, and now, I suppose, it will be in all the Paris papers and be telegraphed over to London. We don't want the business to get into the papers at all if we can help it, but if it must go in, for goodness' sake let it be our version and not a French reporter's."

"I agree with you, sir. We don't want the French Press to report it," said Carruthers with a frown. "But I doubt whether we can stop it now without invoking the help of the people at the Quai d'Orsay, and that would only make things worse when it came out. The next thing would be headlines in the *Paris-Matin*—'SUDDEN DEATH OF A BRITISH DIPLOMATIST. SUICIDE OR A POLITICAL ASSASSINATION?'"

"Good God! Is that what they do here?" The ambassador started up from his chair with a groan and hobbled to his writing-table. He was one of those diplomats *de carrière* who had risen step by step to his present exalted dignity—the last post before his retirement—by doing everything he was told to do faultlessly; by making faultless little speeches on occasions when such speeches are called for; by keeping the Press at arm's length under all circumstances. He was now a man of past sixty and looked his age. He was a hypochondriac, always fussing about his health and generally without reason.

"You see, sir, the French public has been brought up for seven or eight months to believe that every sudden death of a functionary is a political murder. It makes good copy for the sensational newspapers."

"Look here, my dear fellow; somehow this must be stopped. Telephone to Dr. Hoskyn and go with him to the police, and if necessary be present when the post-mortem examination is made. Young Everett may have committed suicide; that would be bad enough; but whatever we do we must keep the gutter Press at arm's length. You might ring me up and let me know how you get on."

Eric Carruthers went down to his own room in the Chancery to use the telephone. He rang up Dr. Hoskyn, whose voice began to flutter when he learned that the call came from the Embassy.

"I hope that you have no bad news about Sir Wilfred," he said.

"No, doctor, but I want you to take a taxi at once and come here and ask for me, Eric Carruthers. I'll tell you why when I see you."

While waiting for his visitor Carruthers sent for the second secretary, Percival Maynard.

"Maynard, the ambassador tells me that you were the first person to receive news of Everett's death. Who brought the news?"

Maynard was a young man with a languid manner, who talked French more fluently than his own language. He was a welcome guest at French luncheon-tables and was a mine of information upon the intrigues in the lobbies of the Chamber and the Senate, and the latest political scandals.

"A police *commissaire*, who said that he came from the ninth *arrondissement*, came in about an hour ago. He had Everett's Embassy card in his hand and he said that the body had been found in Everett's flat, with some sanguinary details. I gathered that he was the man who was first called in by the concierge."

"What did you think of Frank Everett? You saw more of him than I did."

"Everett? Well, he seemed like any other newspaper man that one meets in Fleet Street and avoids if one can—quite a decent young man within his natural limits and, I imagine, fairly good at his job."

Carruthers was drumming on the table with his fingers. His complaint was that one could never get a straight answer out of Maynard.

"Do you know who his friends were?"

"Do you mean here in the Embassy or outside?"

"Both. First, in the Embassy."

"Well, I should think that Ned Gregory saw most of him. I used to hear his voice and his laugh—what a laugh he had, poor devil!—coming from Gregory's room. Gregory's a bit of a wag, as you know."

"So I've heard," observed Carruthers dryly. "Did Everett ever tell you about his people in England?"

"Never. I never asked him. Our intercourse was always on official matters. He was quite well informed about Paris Press matters."

The messenger opened the door to announce Dr. Hoskyn.

Carruthers rose. "Thank you, Maynard. I'm going out with Dr. Hoskyn for an hour or two. Will you mind the baby?"

Dr. Hoskyn was a fussy little man with white hair, purpling cheeks and a soothing, bedside manner. When there was a considerable British colony in Paris, he had had a good private practice and it was natural that he should be called in by the people at the Embassy when a doctor was required.

"Sit down, doctor," said Carruthers, pointing to the chair beside his table. "You've heard, no doubt, of the death of poor Everett, our Press attaché."

The doctor's cheeks deepened in hue. "Dead! That healthy-looking young fellow? What did he die of? An accident?"

"The police give us the choice between suicide and murder. There was a knife wound in the throat. I don't know whether you have had any experience in police medical work, but the ambassador has great confidence in you, and he wants you to make a post-mortem examination of the body and furnish him with an opinion if you can."

"I have never had to do anything of that kind since my old hospital training days," said the doctor doubtfully.

The taxi was announced.

"Come along, doctor," said Carruthers. "I don't know how these things are done in Paris—whether they hold inquests as we do, or whether the police get busy and turn the case over to a *Juge d'Instruction*."

"They will have moved the body down to the Judicial Medical School by this time," said the doctor gloomily.

Carruthers directed the taxi-man to drive them to the police office of the ninth *arrondissement*. There they found a senior police officer and were ushered into his room. Carruthers made the necessary introductions. "This is Dr. Hoskyn, *monsieur le commissaire*, medical officer of the British Embassy, and I am the first secretary. We have called about that distressing case of M. Everett, a member of our staff."

"Ah! You mean the case of the gentleman found dead in an *appartement* in the rue St. Georges this morning." The officer touched a bell-push and a constable made his appearance. "Chairs for these gentlemen."

Two chairs were brought in, dusted and placed at a corner of the table.

"May I inquire, monsieur, whether you have reached any conclusion?" asked Carruthers.

"Monsieur is, of course, aware that the body bore a deep wound in the throat. To judge from the state of the *appartement* it seemed clear that there had been a violent struggle. Furniture was over-turned; a table-lamp was broken and on the floor was lying this knife." He flung open a drawer and took from it a heavy dagger in a sheath with blood-stain upon it; on the blade were engraved the words, "*Blut und Ehre!*"

"These daggers, we understand, are carried by young schoolboys in Germany when they march along the road on the German side of the frontier. You will notice the symbol in the coloured shield on the handle—the swastika in the middle. It is Hitler's device for fostering a warlike spirit among German schoolboys."

Carruthers examined the weapon, which was about a foot long. The blade was stained with dried blood. He passed it to Dr. Hoskyn who said, "Does this mean that young Everett was murdered by a German?"

"We do not know, monsieur. When the *concierge* was interrogated she said that when dusting the *appartement* she had often noticed this dagger lying on the table in the sitting-room. It must have belonged to M. Everett himself."

"I believe it did," said Carruthers. "I remember hearing that Mr. Everett had displayed a dagger like this to his colleagues in the Embassy. He said that a journalistic colleague on the frontier had sent it to him to use as a paper-knife."

"We should be grateful, monsieur, if that could be verified. It will help us in reconstructing the case. This much we know already from the *concierge*: Mr. Everett had arranged with her that she should prepare his *petit déjeuner* every morning and bring it up to the door of his *appartement*; then she would knock and set down the tray. Sometimes he opened the door and took it from her; more often it stayed for some minutes on the landing before he took it in. It was so this morning. She left the breakfast on the landing and went downstairs to her other duties. When she went up to do her dusting the breakfast was still lying untouched. She knocked repeatedly but could get no answer, and on opening the door was shocked to find that her tenant was lying fully dressed on the floor. She thought at first that he had had some kind of seizure and that in falling he had pulled the table over him; but on going to the body she saw blood on the floor, and she left the body as it was and ran down to telephone to us. As I told you the room was in the utmost disorder, and so much blood on the floor that they thought Mr. Everett must have bled to death. The *concierge* did not think that Mr. Everett brought anyone back with him last night and she heard no one go upstairs."

"You have formed a theory, monsieur?"

The officer spread his forearms wide. "We have not yet had time to consider theories beyond this: at some time after the poor gentleman returned to his *appartement* he received a visitor—a person who must have known him well or he would have had to make inquiries of the *concierge*. For some reason yet to be ascertained there must have been a quarrel; one of them must have attacked the other and in the struggle that ensued the visitor must have snatched up this dagger and plunged it point first into his adversary's throat. Then he must have shut the door behind him as gently as possible and made off without awaking the *concierge*. At present officers are searching the *appartement* for finger-prints, but these seldom lead to identifications, unless they were made by some well-known criminal. I do not think that this crime was the work of any known criminal."

"Where is the body now?"

"It has been taken to the Medico-legal School. If you desire to see it I will send one of my officers with you."

"I should be very glad if you would. I was hoping that you would allow Dr. Hoskyn to join your medical officer in making the autopsy."

The *commissaire* bowed politely. "That does not rest with me, monsieur, but with the authorities of the School; but I imagine that they would be very glad to avail themselves of Dr. Hoskyn's good offices. I will inquire."

"I suppose that you have not yet had time to look through the papers found on Mr. Everett's body or in the *appartement*?"

"I have them all here, monsieur, including a number of notes and coins which no ordinary thief would have left behind him. I shall not fail to present a copy of my report to his Excellency the ambassador when it is complete. Now, if you are going to the School I think it might be wise for you to go there early. I will ring up our police surgeon and arrange to meet you there."

The laboratory attached to the Medico-legal School is the most depressing spot in Paris. It seems always to be tenanted; the bodies of the unrecognized are laid on sloping slate slabs behind plate-glass windows. The public, who come to look for missing friends, pass in front of the windows, where they may find their nearest and dearest lying exposed to the general gaze like the wares in a fishmonger's shop.

A youngish man in a black wide-awake hat, who appeared to have been waiting in the doorway, came forward as the taxi pulled up. He swept off his imposing headgear, disclosing a domed head polished like a billiard ball, and introduced himself as Dr. Audusson, a professor of the School. Leading the way into the building, the police officer explained to him the object of the visit of the two Englishmen, and they were taken straight into the room fitted up for post-mortem examinations. There, covered by a sheet, lay the body of Carruthers' late colleague. The sheet was stripped off, disclosing the body dressed in its ordinary day clothes, which were stiffened and discoloured by extravasated blood. Dr. Audusson clicked his tongue and observed to his British colleague that the cause of death was not far to seek. He pointed to the deep incision in the throat. The two professional men consulted in an undertone, and then Dr. Hoskyn came over to Carruthers.

"I suppose that the ambassador wants a complete post-mortem. He wouldn't be satisfied by a report that that wound in itself would account for the death?"

Carruthers had his share of Scottish caution. "The question of drug-taking or poison might arise hereafter. I think that it would be wise to cover all points."

"Very well; my French colleague is quite willing. and we shall have the help of the public laboratory for analysing the contents of the stomach."

"Then you won't want me any more?"

"No. As soon as the examination is completed I will come on to the Embassy with my report."

"You won't forget the possibility of suicide, doctor?"

"We will not."

Carruthers had scarcely shut the door of his room when Maynard, the second secretary, entered with care graven on his features.

"I'm glad you're back," he said; "I've had a perfectly awful time with the old man upstairs. He expects everything to be done at lightning speed—made me telegraph to Everett's next-of-kin to announce the death, and I suppose that now we shall have a tribe of them on our backs. Then the ambassador wanted me to account for every moment of Everett's time, and I had to tell him that I knew very little about the poor fellow, but that I would find out as much as was known about him."

"You're lucky not to have the place beset by reporters."

"Oh, we've had them by the dozen. I refused to see them. I told Gregory to shoo them out. He must have done the job effectively, for they've left us alone for nearly half an hour."

"Gregory is the man who knew Everett best, isn't he?"

"Yes; he saw more of him than we did."

"Let's have him in."

Maynard left the room and returned with the third secretary.

"Sit down, Gregory, and tell us all you knew about poor Everett."

Ned Gregory was a curly-headed youngster with red hair. He was trying to discipline his features to the expression which he imagined to be suitable for funerals, but it was an effort; the natural levity in his vivacious eyes was difficult to subdue.

"When did you last see him?" continued Carruthers.

"Yesterday morning. I used to see him practically every morning."

"You knew him pretty well, I suppose?"

"Fairly well. I never went out with him, but he used to tell me a lot about his job."

"Was he sometimes depressed?"

A cloud crossed Gregory's eyes for a moment.

"He used to confide in me a lot, but he seemed generally to be in good spirits."

"Always?" Carruthers had not missed the momentary cloud.

"Always, except once. I don't like betraying the poor fellow's confidence."

"I quite understand, but with this mystery about his death…"

"Well, he was very much in love with a French girl he had met somewhere or other. He told me that he intended to marry her. I tried to dissuade him, and then, much to my surprise, he came in yesterday morning and told me that it was all off—that he'd found out the girl was a married woman. He seemed to be very hard hit. He wanted my advice as to whether he ought to break with her entirely. I told him that if it was my case I should. He said that if he dropped her like a hot potato she would feel it acutely; she had told him that she hated her husband."

The two secretaries exchanged glances, and Carruthers said, "Thank you, Gregory. If you remember anything else that would tend to clear up Everett's death, please come and see me."

"There's one thing I should like to ask before I go. Does the French Penal Code prohibit the use of man-traps for journalists? You never saw such a crew as I've had here this afternoon— camera men as well as reporters. If I'm led away with gyves upon my wrists it will be because I've sent one or two of them to the place where they belong."

"Maynard tells me that you've been very successful with them..."

Before Gregory had time to reply the messenger opened the door. "There's some more reporters asking for you, Mr. Gregory," he said.

Ned Gregory threw up his hands and disappeared.

"What he's just told us, Maynard, cuts both ways. It might have been murder by an injured husband or it might equally have been a suicide."

Chapter Two

CARRUTHERS ran upstairs to see the ambassador. He found him querulous and impatient. "I've been waiting all the afternoon for your telephone message and for word from someone who knows what has been happening."

"There was really nothing to tell you, sir, that I could not do quicker by returning to the Embassy. Dr. Hoskyn and I saw the body in the Institute of Legal Medicine, which has taken the place of the Morgue, with the French police doctor. I left the two doctors to make the post-mortem examination together. I asked them to make their report as full as possible."

"Couldn't they say offhand what was the cause of death?"

"Yes, sir. Everett had been stabbed deeply in the throat with a German dagger—one of those Nazi weapons with which German schoolboys are armed. The police showed us the dagger stained with blood."

"Do you mean that the crime was done by a German Nazi?"

"No, sir; the dagger belonged to Everett himself. It had been sent to him by a friend on the other side of the frontier. But just now young Gregory told me that Everett used to confide in him about an unfortunate love-affair with a French girl. He wanted to marry her and she seemed willing, but somehow he discovered that she was a married woman and that her husband was alive. Gregory says that he advised him strongly never to see her again, but it struck me as possible—"

"You mean that the murderer may have been an injured husband?"

Carruthers nodded; his chief groaned and fell back in his chair. "Why do they saddle us with newspaper men? It's a legacy from the old bad days of the war. If the Press gets hold of this..."

A light tap on the door; Chubb entered with the latest edition of the newspapers and retired discreetly, after winking covertly at Carruthers and jerking his thumb towards the topmost journal. Chubb considered himself a privileged person. He had been an N.C.O. of exemplary character during the war, and had since served three ambassadors. He judged men as he found them, without much consideration of their official rank.

The ambassador was fidgeting in his chair. If he had been alone it was obvious that he would have pounced hungrily on the papers and scanned their headlines. It was cruel to keep him in suspense; Carruthers snatched up the topmost print and read it with curling lip.

"What do they say?" asked his chief.

"The usual sensational garbage on which these papers live. 'British Embassy Mystery.' 'The Crime in the Rue St. Georges.'"

The ambassador ran his eye down the column with quick-coming breath. "Scandalous! Have they no decency, these cursed reporters? What's this? 'The secretary swallowed his fifth cup of tea before replying to my question. "The mysterious Mademoiselle X," he said. "No, I can tell you nothing about her."' Which of the staff drinks five cups of tea?"

"Gregory saw the man, I believe, and hunted him out, and Gregory hates tea. The whole article must have been concocted in the office."

"Yes, and it will be quoted in the English papers. Now I suppose these jackals will hunt the woman down and magnify the business into a political crime, bringing in incidentally the names of one or two French Ministers. By the way, I sent a sympathetic telegram to Everett's father this afternoon. Maynard found the address in the boy's papers. I suppose some of the family will come out. Of course I telegraphed also to the Foreign Office, and, talking of the F.O., how would it be to suggest to them that a man from the C.I.D. in Scotland Yard be sent over to make independent inquiries?"

"I shouldn't do that just yet, sir. The principal *commissaire* that I saw seemed to be taking an intelligent line about the case, and if the French police solve the mystery we shall be glad that we kept out of it."

"Perhaps you're right. When Dr. Hoskyn comes in, please send him up to me."

In his room Carruthers found another copy of the *Paris-Matin* spread out on his writing-table; Chubb had even taken the liberty of marking the column. It was certainly a startling testimony to the enterprise of the Paris journalist, according to whom Everett had been seen two nights before, taking leave of a maiden of astonishing beauty outside the Café Weber, and tears were coursing down the lady's damask cheek. "Who was this fair unknown whom we will call Mademoiselle X? Had she anything to do with the crime in the rue St. Georges? Was she another Mata Hari?"

Chubb entered the room at this moment, bringing the usual cup of tea.

"You've been having a busy day, Chubb—with these journalists and people?"

"It's not the reporters I mind so much—Mr. Gregory deals with them and they go out faster than they came in. It's these camera men I object to—the saucy blokes. Fancy them holding up their cameras to take a shot of me on the doorstep. What's the sense of it?"

"They have their living to make like everybody else," observed Carruthers.

"If I had my way with them, sir, they'd be getting their living chained to an oar in the galleys in Cayenne with a cloud of mosquitoes gnawing at them. Why, what do you think one of them did this afternoon? Came in with a pair of opera-glasses, he did, and looked through them at the blank wall in the courtyard. '*Ca y est!*' he said, and grinned at me. 'What do you mean?' I said. Then he showed me. While he was looking at the blank wall he was taking a photograph of me through a little trap-door at the side. He told me I'd be in all the papers to-morrow. There ought to be a law about it."

"You might ask Mr. Gregory to look in here for a moment."

"Right, sir. He's just thrown out a gang of these reporters, but there's more waiting to see him."

"He can leave the others to Mr. Dundas. I shan't keep him a minute."

Ned Gregory looked a little dishevelled and heated when he made his appearance.

"I'm sorry to disturb you in your important diplomatic labours, Gregory, but you may not have seen this," showing him the lines about the maiden of startling beauty at the Café Weber. "I suppose they did not get a hint about this woman from you?"

"Good Lord, no! One of them had the impudence to mention this to me, and I told him plainly that if he shoved in any inaccuracy he'd be for it."

"What! You threatened him?"

"I did, but it wasn't the kind of threat that he'd dare to publish."

"What was it then?"

"Well, I'm getting to know quite a lot about the ins and outs of the Paris Press. *Paris-Matin* has a mortal enemy—the *Courrier du Midi*—so I told this blighter that if he didn't mind his step I'd shove a *démenti* into the columns of the *Courrier*: that made him sit up. He comes and feeds out of my hand now."

"Well, don't go too far with them, or you may find that you've started a dead set against us and there'll be a pained inquiry from the Foreign Office asking who's responsible, and you may be offered up. Did you gather what was likely to be their line now?"

"Yes, they're all running the scent of the mysterious Mademoiselle X. There's nothing we can do to stop them, unless we get the Quai d'Orsay to muzzle them. There's some unholy pact between the Government and the Press in this country. A word from the mandarins on the other side of the river would stop the whole thing. One of these fellows seems to have got wind of that German dagger stunt, and if they run that for all it's worth, Everett will be turned into a German spy in the British Embassy."

"The Lord forfend it! It would be the death of the ambassador!"

Dr. Hoskyn bustled into the room. "I'm afraid I haven't anything very definite to tell you yet, but everything is in train. When I left they were applying the laboratory tests to the stomach and digestive organs, and that far the result was negative. I shall have the final report late this evening or early to-morrow morning."

"If you don't mind coming up, doctor, we'll tell the ambassador; he's in rather a nervous state about this business and you may be able to soothe him."

They found Sir Wilfred Bryant at his table. He was plainly in a nervous state, but he laid down his pen on seeing who his visitors were. "You're just in time, doctor. I'm drafting a dispatch to the Foreign Office telling them how the matter stands. I shall try to get it away to-night, because the correspondents of the English papers are sure to telephone the news of the death. I am saying that in the opinion of the police it was a case of murder."

"I think," said Hoskyn, "that we can quite dismiss the theory of suicide. If a man attempts suicide with a pointed weapon he plunges it into his chest, not into his throat; if he injures his throat at all he tries to cut it with a sharp blade in a sawing fashion."

The ambassador shuddered and cowered in his chair; if Hoskyn had a fault, he thought, it was in bluntness of speech.

"Besides," continued Hoskyn, "the police described to us the state of the room—chairs and tables thrown over, lamp lying smashed on the floor, all the marks of a violent struggle. They had gone some way towards reconstructing the crime. The late visitor had not been unknown to Everett because Everett had let him in. As far as they could judge there had been no robbery, because the contents of Everett's pockets had not been taken. For some reason the men had quarrelled; the visitor had snatched up this German dagger and had plunged it into his victim's throat while he was lying on the ground. I may say that in the course of the post-mortem we found evidence that the deceased had received more than one blow in the face from a fist."

"You will let me have a complete report of the post-mortem as early as you can, Dr. Hoskyn? Everett's parents may be over here to-morrow, and we ought to be in a position to tell them all that is known."

"You shall have it at the earliest possible moment, Sir Wilfred," said the doctor as he followed Carruthers out of the room.

Chubb met them at the bottom of the stairs and told Carruthers that a police officer was waiting to see him.

"Bring him into my room," said Carruthers, shaking hands with the doctor.

The policeman was in plain clothes. He was a nice-looking, pleasant-spoken man of between thirty and forty. He saluted and took the chair indicated by Carruthers.

"I should explain, monsieur, that I am the officer charged with the inquiry into the murder in the rue St. Georges, Inspector Bigot. My chief thought it well that you should be informed of the latest development, and that you should be asked to help up as far as you can in following a new line of inquiry."

"Have you traced the woman mentioned in the newspapers as Mademoiselle X?"

"We have, monsieur; indeed she herself came to the station to ask whether what she had seen in the papers was true. I myself took a statement from her."

Carruthers leaned forward. "What type of woman was she?"

"A perfectly respectable young married woman, monsieur, the wife of a civil servant stationed in Algiers. Her father is a retired business man who was able to give her a considerable dot at her marriage. It was clear to us that she was very much attached to M. Everett."

"How did they first meet?"

"At the first night of a new French film, where the house was filled with critics and journalists. She had been taken there by a journalist friend who knew M. Everett well. He presented him to the lady. Unfortunately, it seems he called her 'mademoiselle', and did not explain her real name and position to Mr. Everett, who seemed to think that she was unmarried. That was the starting-point."

"How long ago was this?"

"A little over two months ago; we verified the date at the Cinema House."

"And they met frequently afterwards?"

"Very frequently. If her story is correct, they met every day; sometimes for lunch, sometimes to dine and go to the theatre together. He proposed marriage to her, and then learned for the first time that she had a husband."

"Ah!"

"We thought that perhaps this was a crime of passion, of jealousy on the part of the husband, but no. Inquiries made at the Ministry show that the husband is still in Algiers and therefore could not possibly have been in Paris at the time of the murder."

"Had she any other admirer who might have been jealous of Mr. Everett?"

"I think not, monsieur. She was very much attached to Mr. Everett, and if she had had any suspicion of a possible murderer she would have been anxious to bring him to justice."

There was a pause. Bigot dropped his voice mysteriously. "I have come to inquire whether the late Mr. Everett was employed by your Secret Service to make reports upon German re-armament?"

Carruthers showed his astonishment. "Certainly not, *monsieur le commissaire*. Anything of that kind was quite outside his functions."

"Of course you will understand that anything that you tell me will be treated as entirely confidential."

"If he had been engaged in any work of that kind I should not hesitate to tell you. His duties were of a routine character."

"You may not be aware, monsieur, that the weapon used in the assassination was a German Nazi dagger, ground to a fine edge and bearing the words in German, 'Blood and Glory'; the swastika device is on its handle. This certainly suggests that it was a political murder."

"It might suggest that to anyone who was not aware that the dagger in question belonged to Mr. Everett himself; that he had had it in his apartment for weeks past, and that his concierge had seen it every morning when she dusted his sitting-room."

"I am aware of that, monsieur; I am aware also of the fact that the weapon was sent to Mr. Everett by a friend on the other side of the frontier, but it has occurred to me that in sending this dagger Mr. Everett's friend hoped that it would be used as anti-German propaganda, and that the Germans have heard of it and have taken their usual remedy by secretly murdering the owner of the dagger."

If the matter had not been so serious Carruthers would have laughed at the fantastic credulity even of French officials. He decided to give a grave warning to the man. "So far," he said, "the reporters who have called at the Embassy know nothing about this German dagger. You yourself know that if they get hold of that there will be no end to the inventions of the newspapers. The murderer will become a German spy sent to steal a document of the highest importance; the cry will be taken up by the entire Press; we who know how the dagger came into France shall be accused of hiding the truth. I hope earnestly that nothing will be said about the dagger to any journalist who may call at the police station."

"You need have no fear of that, monsieur."

In spite of this comforting assurance there was something in the man's manner that made Carruthers uneasy. Bigot tried to cover his retreat.

"Could Mr. Everett have had any important official paper about him which other journalists might covet?"

"No, I can reassure you on that point; it was no part of his duty to carry secret papers out of the Embassy. In fact, no secret papers passed through his hands."

The brigadier rose to take his leave. Carruthers shook hands with him and opened the door to show him out. He narrowly escaped colliding with Gregory, who was on his way in with an open newspaper in his hand. He was unusually excited.

"I want you to look at this." He produced the latest edition of *Le Témoin* and pointed to the headlines in heavy type.

"ASSASSINATION OF A BRITISH DIPLOMAT

"WAS IT THE WORK OF THE GERMAN REICH?
"Dagger inscribed 'Blut und Ehre' (Blood and Glory)

"It has just come to the knowledge of one of our collaborators that the weapon used in the crime in the rue St. Georges was a German Nazi dagger bearing the swastika badge on its hilt and the words *'Blut und Ehre'* engraved on the blade; that it had been ground to a sharp cutting edge with a needle point. The empty sheath of this formidable weapon was found on the table; the dagger itself was lying on the floor beside the body, stained with the dried blood of the victim. The medico-legal experts are now investigating the cause of death and we understand that the wound in the throat of the unfortunate British diplomat was almost certainly caused by a stab from this dagger. It is for the British Government to take the first step, but it must not be forgotten that the crime was committed on French soil and it will be for the French Government to demand satisfaction for an outrage which has taken place in France against a representative of a friendly ally."

"Good Lord! The ambassador will never get over this. How could that reporter have got hold of it? That police commissary said that they were as anxious as we were that nothing should get into the Press, but I didn't believe him."

"The ambassador will have to be told and the news must be broken to him gently. I suppose you will see to that?"

"I suppose I must," muttered Carruthers gloomily.

With the paper in his hand he was half-way up the stairs when he met the ambassador coming down.

"I was coming down to see you, Carruthers," he said. "Let us go up to my room. I've sent the draft of my dispatch down to the Chancery; I should like you to look through it and see that it covers all the ground."

"I will, sir. I was coming up to show you this that has just been brought to me."

The ambassador read it with a sharp intake of his breath.

"That settles it. Please telegraph to the Foreign Office saying that in my opinion a competent French-speaking officer should be sent over from Scotland Yard to assist the French police. This is going to be a horrible business for us all."

Chapter Three

AMONG THE various changes entailed by re-organization at Scotland Yard had been the translation of Morden to a vast room on the first floor, and the dispersal of the senior staff of the central C.I.D. body to various rooms in other parts of the building. Morden's messenger entered, carrying the printed form which visitors to the building are required to fill up, together with a visiting-card on which the name, "Mr. Ralph Nugent, Foreign Office," was inscribed.

"Where is he?" asked Morden.

"Just outside, sir. As I knew you would see him I brought him upstairs with me."

"Show him in."

Mr. Nugent proved to be a tall young man, irreproachably groomed and tailored. He was the latest recruit to the office which conducts diplomatic correspondence with the country's representatives abroad, and is gently pushed aside in a crisis to make room for the men of action that Ministers imagine themselves to be until they find their level in the talking-shop at Geneva.

"I've come on rather a delicate mission," explained Nugent. "Our ambassador in Paris has asked for the help of one of your officers who can speak French."

"Why, has somebody been robbing the Embassy till?"

"Worse than that, I'm sorry to say. Somebody has been unkind enough to murder a member of the Embassy staff."

"I saw something about it in this morning's paper. Surely the Paris police are at work on the case."

"They are, but apparently that does not satisfy the ambassador. He seems to be afraid that the Paris papers will try to turn the case into another political scandal like the '*Prince affaire.*' That was all worked up by the newspapers."

"Our men proved to their own satisfaction that it was a suicide."

"And so they did to the French police, but the French police do not dare to say so for fear of being accused of being in the scandal themselves. My instructions are to ask you unofficially whether you would lend us a man, nominally to help the Paris police, actually to find out who committed the murder and why. The French police have already gone off the deep end by trying to connect the death with a Nazi plan of revenge, on the strength of a Nazi dagger which had been in the man's possession for months. If we know that your reply will be in the affirmative, an official letter to the Commissioner will follow."

Morden reflected, drumming with his fingers on the table. "There will be the question of his expenses..." He said.

"Those would be met from Foreign Office funds."

"Our men hunt in couples; there would have to be two of them."

"I fancy we could run to that too."

"If the Commissioner agrees, the man I should send is one of our younger inspectors who has done work in France before. He does not speak French, but the man who would go with him is fairly proficient. If you will sit tight for a moment I will speak to the Commissioner."

Nugent had not long to wait. In two minutes Morden returned to say that all was serene; that the official letter could be sent over whenever the Foreign Office pleased.

"I am sure to be asked the name of the man you will send."

"The leader of the expeditionary corps will be Inspector Richardson. His second will probably be Sergeant Cooper, who speaks French fluently."

As soon as Morden was left alone he rang for the superintendent of the Central Division.

"The Foreign Office is going to ask for officers to work in Paris for a few days, Mr. Longden; to work with the French police on that case you may have seen in the papers—the murder of the Press attaché to the Embassy. Has Richardson anything important on hand?"

The superintendent wrinkled his brow. He was considering less what Richardson had on hand than what his seniors would say if their junior were given a trip to Paris at the public expense. "Richardson doesn't speak much French, sir," he objected.

"Quite true, but I thought of sending Sergeant Cooper as his understudy, and Cooper speaks French quite well. Besides, Richardson ran that Liverpool solicitor, Maze, to ground through the evidence he got in France without any cost to the department. We mustn't forget that."

"Very good, sir. Shall I warn him to be ready?"

"Not yet. We have to wait for an official letter from the Foreign Office. All I want you to do is to avoid putting Richardson or Cooper on to any new case."

The official letter was brought over by hand the same afternoon; the train for the night boat carried Richardson and Cooper over to France, each armed with a certificate from the Foreign Office describing the bearer as attached to the Embassy in Paris, in lieu of a passport. Actually, the superintendent had understated Richardson's proficiency in French. Ever since the Maze case the junior inspector in "Central" had devoted all his evenings to a study of the language, and had joined a class in French conversation conducted by a French lady from Tours. His ambition was to burst upon the department as a French interpreter as soon as he felt sure of himself. Only Sergeant Cooper knew this, and he was bound to secrecy. During the waking hours of their journey, Richardson insisted that French should be their only language.

Arrived at St. Lazare, they left their luggage in the cloak-room and swallowed an early breakfast in the café at the end of the Galerie des Pas Perdus, where Cooper studied the columns of Paris-Matin to see what the Paris newspapers were saying about the murder.

"Mr. Morden wasn't far wrong in what he told us about these Paris papers. Listen to this.

"'THE ASSASSINATION OF THE BRITISH DIPLOMAT

"'The plot is thickening. It is now known that the body of the British diplomat, M. Everett, bore on the left cheek the well-known symbol of the German Nazi secret police, scratched with the point of a dagger. This mark is always made on the corpses of the Nazi victims, even when their relations are told that the victim was shot during an attempt to escape. One can well understand why; it is to inspire terror.'

"There's a lot more of it, and half a column about the mysterious Mademoiselle X, whose identity, they say, is not yet known. The paper suggests that she is the mistress of one of the Cabinet Ministers, and that he is shielding her."

"The worst of it is that the readers of the paper swallow all this stuff, and one can never overtake the lies they tell." Richardson consulted his watch. "If we're going to walk to the Embassy we had better be starting. It is nearly ten."

Cooper knew the way to the Faubourg St. Honoré. In fifteen minutes they found themselves opposite the imposing front of the British Embassy, and crossed the street to ring the bell. Four or five young men appeared to be on guard at the big iron gate. One of them accosted Cooper as a *confrère*.

"You will pardon me, monsieur, if I ask you what English paper you represent."

Cooper's expression was a picture of non-comprehension; he shrugged his shoulders and shook his head. The man fell back, and they reached the bell unmolested. The porter examined their papers and opened the gate just wide enough to admit them.

"You are a little early, gentlemen," he said. "They don't keep early hours here, but if you'll step over to the Chancery and tell them who you are they'll let you in."

The man who actually received them was Chubb, the incorrigible non-respecter of persons. "Detective officers from Scotland Yard, are you? I don't know that I've ever come across one before except, of course, in the books. Well, you're going to find your work cut out for you here"—he jerked his thumb in the direction of the Chancery—"they've all gone gaga over there from the old man downwards—all except Mr. Gregory; he knows how to tell these reporter chaps where they get off."

"There's a lot of them waiting outside the gate now," observed Cooper.

"You bet your life there are. If you let them in and don't tell them anything, they go away and invent lies. That's where Mr.

Gregory steps in. He does the innocent child stunt. Instead of letting them interview *him*, he sucks their brains—all in their own lingo—and sends them away happy. Damn it, he'll be glad you've come over! But I oughtn't to keep you standing here. I'll take you along to the waiting-room. Mr. Gregory will be in directly."

Chubb had three manners—the formal manner of respect which he kept for the ambassador and the first secretary; the manner of the privileged dependant which was reserved for other members of the Embassy staff; and the manner and speech of the sergeants' mess. For detectives he adopted instinctively the second of these; the expeditionary corps from Scotland Yard were destined, at a later stage of their acquaintance, to enjoy the third, which would have struck them as odd coming from the lips of a man whose breast was emblazoned with the ribbons of war medals, for Chubb had been in the South African as well as the Great War, and had greatly distinguished himself in both.

In the waiting-room Richardson proceeded to draw out his new acquaintance.

"What were the duties of the Press attaché?" was his first question.

"Ah, there you have me. I don't believe anyone knew, unless Mr. Carruthers, the first secretary, did. He had a pile of French newspapers to go through every morning, and I had them afterwards for lighting the stove in winter. Then he'd go out, generally for the rest of the day. What he did in the town is more than I can tell you, but it seemed to be a soft job, whatever it was."

"What kind of a man was he?"

"Oh, a civil-spoken young fellow, always ready to pass the time of day, but not one of the brainy sort, if you know what I mean."

"Did he have many visitors here?"

"Not one. Any people that he saw he must have met somewhere in the town. The papers are saying that he had a young woman—Miss X, they call her—but in France they always drag a woman into every case you read of. Their public's been brought up to expect it. I believe that they keep a stock of good-looking girls on their staff to pose for their photographs as the mystery woman in the case—Mademoiselle X…hullo, I believe I hear someone. I'll run along and see whether it's Mr. Gregory."

In less than two minutes Chubb returned, arrayed in his official manners. "If you'll step this way, gentlemen, Mr. Gregory will be pleased to receive you."

"You've arrived a day before we expected you," said Gregory. "It was quick work."

"Yes, sir, we had rather short notice, but we caught last night's boat train."

"Did you happen to notice when you came in whether any reporters were hanging about the gate?"

"Yes, sir," replied Cooper; "there were half a dozen or so. They must have been reporters, because one of them claimed me as a *confrère*, and asked me what English newspaper I represented."

"What did you tell him?"

"I'm afraid that I pretended not to understand him."

"But you do speak French?"

"Yes, sir, but not well enough to pass for a Frenchman."

"Sergeant Cooper is too modest, sir; he is our French interpreter at the Yard."

"Good, then we needn't waste time by discussing the case. I propose to take you both down to the *commissaire* who is in charge of the investigations. You must not let out to him that you are officially sent by the Foreign Office. I shall explain that the ambassador had asked you to come over to act as liaison officers between the Paris police and the Embassy; in fact, to make yourselves generally useful under direction; and you should ask particularly that your presence here should not be divulged to any French reporter. You might hint in the course of conversation that you would be in a position to answer any question that may arise about the official duties of the late Mr. Everett. By the way, I ought to tell you that a post-mortem was made on the body yesterday, and that no trace was found of poison or drugs. The cause of death was a stab in the throat which penetrated the carotid artery. My only other news is that the ambassador has had a telegram from Everett's father that he and the mother are coming over to-day."

"Very good, sir; we are ready to start whenever you like."

Gregory went to the door and shouted for Chubb, who came bustling down the passage.

"Look here, Chubb; just run up to the servants' bedroom on the second floor and take a squint at the railings. You might count the blighters who are waiting for the gate to be opened. You have the key of the garden gate, haven't you?"

"Yes, Mr. Gregory. I see what you want; you want to do a bolt into the Champs-Élysées."

"Only if the coast isn't clear."

"I can tell you that without busting myself to go up to any second-floor window. There's a regular army of them this morning."

"Right then, we'll execute a strategic retreat, Chubb."

Armed with the key of the postern, Chubb led the way through the pleasant Embassy garden to the bolt-hole used by the gardeners. "I won't go out and call a taxi for you, Mr. Gregory, because that would attract attention."

The three hunted men walked for fifty yards before hailing a passing taxi. Gregory directed the driver to set them down at the junction between the rue de Lafayette and the rue de Châteaudun. From there they walked to the police station of the *arrondissement,* taking care to see that no one was following them and that no journalist was on guard at the door, nor on the opposite side of the street.

"All clear," said Gregory, after a quick scrutiny. "We'll walk boldly in and ask to see the superintendent in charge of the *arrondissement*."

The constable on duty at the door seemed a little surprised at their demand and asked the nature of their business. Gregory smiled knowingly and said, "I can assure you that the superintendent will ask for nothing better than to see us. You might show him this card," he added, tendering a visiting-card bearing the address, "British Embassy."

In less than a minute they were ushered into the room of the functionary, who rose to receive them.

"Be seated, gentlemen."

"I come from the British Embassy, monsieur," said Gregory.

"And these gentlemen, monsieur?"

"They come from Scotland Yard, monsieur. Detective Inspector Richardson and Detective Sergeant Cooper. The ambassador thought that they would be useful to you in the examination of documents in English, and as liaison officers between you and the Embassy. They will put themselves entirely under your orders for any duty that you may care to entrust them with. If you have no need for their services you have only to say so."

"On the contrary, monsieur, they will be of the greatest use to us, presuming that they understand French."

"Both officers speak French. They are ready to get to work at once. The ambassador would be glad, however, if you would arrange that nothing should be said to any French reporter about either of these gentlemen coming from Scotland Yard, or being police officers."

"You may rely upon that, monsieur; they shall be merely interpreters attached to the Embassy."

The superintendent threw open his door and sent a passing constable for M. Bigot. The three Englishmen had risen.

"This is the officer with whom you will be dealing, messieurs—Inspector Bigot."

The inspector shook hands with Gregory, saying, "I had the pleasure of meeting this gentleman at the British Embassy on Wednesday." He looked inquiringly at the other two. "And these gentlemen?"

"Interpreters and translators attached to the Embassy," said Gregory laconically. "They are prepared to begin their duties at once."

"Good," said Bigot; "then I will take them to my room."

The three shook hands with the superintendent and were conducted along the passage to the little room assigned to the inspector, who threw open the door and invited them to pass him. They found that they were not alone in the room. A sharp-faced young man with a note-book and pencil was sitting half hidden by the door. He was writing, but rose on the irruption of the visitors. Bigot, who brought up the rear, was the last to catch sight of him. He uttered an exclamation of annoyance.

"I beg pardon, monsieur, for having entered your room without ceremony," said the young man, "but I have several questions to ask you. Let me inquire first, who are these gentlemen?"

"English friends of mine," replied Bigot shortly.

"Ah, I recognize one of them—the gentleman who receives us journalists at the Embassy. Is it not so, monsieur?" he added, turning to Gregory. "Ah, we are well met on neutral ground here. You can say to me what you would not care to say to a crowd of other journalists"—he sank his voice to the confidential note—"you can tell me, for example, something that will greatly interest my editor. That dagger, now—"

Bigot interrupted brusquely. "I beg your pardon, monsieur. I must remind you that you have no right to walk uninvited into my room, and that I am at present engaged and can answer no questions."

"But surely you can tell me why these gentlemen are here, monsieur?"

"I can answer no questions at all," said Bigot sternly.

Gregory advanced a step, and sinking his voice to a confidential manner said, "I can satisfy your curiosity, monsieur. I have brought these gentlemen here to obtain their identity cards."

"But...!" exclaimed the journalist.

"Not another word, monsieur—I have given you exclusive information that has been given to no other journalist in Paris. More than that, you are quite at liberty to publish this exclusive information. And now, if you will permit me..." He pulled the door open and held it for the journalist to take his departure.

Having expelled the intrusive visitor, Gregory also took his leave. "I can safely leave these gentlemen with you, monsieur, and if they are set upon by journalists in the street outside, I can rely upon you to give them protection."

Inspector Bigot now conducted the two English detectives into a room lined with cupboards, and brought chairs to the long oak table at which a police officer was digging into an untidy pile of papers. He sent the man away and then planked down upon the table another pile, which had been brought down from the dead man's flat.

"There, gentlemen, is your first task. Kindly put on one side any papers that you consider likely to throw light on the identity or the motive of the assassin."

Chapter Four

THE SORTING of a pile of documents was a familiar task to both Richardson and his junior. They sat opposite to one another with the pile between them and began by weeding out all carbon copies of journalistic matter; this they put aside: it reduced the height of the pile to manageable proportions. There remained a heterogeneous mass of papers—notes of invitation in their envelopes, receipted bills, and notes made in French and English on the flyleaves of letters and the backs of envelopes. Like most journalists the dead man seemed to have no method in filing his correspondence or news-cuttings; they were allowed to accumulate to the point when all were destroyed in a common holocaust. There was a series of love-letters in a French feminine hand—doubtless that of the "Mademoiselle X" of whom the newspapers were making so much.

After an hour and a half the first classification had been made. It had been singularly barren. Sergeant Cooper had put aside one letter to which he attached importance. He translated it verbally to Richardson.

"'DEAR FRIEND,

"'Circumstances have arisen making it impossible that the information I gave you yesterday should be communicated to your Embassy. The gentleman in question has now given a satisfactory explanation of his visit to the rue Odéon. I must insist that you destroy in my presence the note that I gave you. I shall come round in person to your *appartment* this evening to see with my own eyes that it is destroyed. This is also the wish of my editor.

"'Your friend,

"'P.C.'"

"Is there no date?" asked Richardson.

"None, except the word 'Tuesday.' It might have been any Tuesday."

"No postmark?"

"None; apparently it was left by hand."

"The *concierge* may remember something about it. He begins 'Dear Friend,' so Mr. Everett must have known him well. I think we ought to get hold of Inspector Bigot. See whether you can dig him out."

The process of "digging out" did not take long. Bigot came in with amused curiosity written on his features. He read the letter with a frown. "Tuesday? The crime was committed on Tuesday."

"You will excuse my question, monsieur," said Richardson, "but did you bring from the flat the scraps of paper from the waste-paper-basket?"

"No, monsieur. I don't even know that there was any waste-paper-basket in the flat."

"Bad searching," murmured Richardson in English. "Ask him whether we could visit the flat together; otherwise there is the danger that the *concierge* may destroy valuable evidence unintentionally."

"I should be at your service, messieurs," said Bigot with a smile, "if we had all eaten. It is now long past our usual hour for lunch. Perhaps you English detectives make a rule of eating nothing until your case is complete, but now that you are in France it becomes a duty to satisfy your appetites."

The Englishmen exchanged a word or two in their own language. "Monsieur," said Richardson, "you would be very good if you would consent to lunch with us. You, no doubt, are aware of the best restaurant in this neighbourhood."

Bigot's eyes glistened. "I know a little restaurant quite close to this police station—the Restaurant des Gourmets."

"Excellent," said Richardson, "you must be our guide." In an undertone to Cooper he said in English, "If it breaks us we shall have to do it."

"The Embassy pays," murmured Cooper.

They caught up their hats and followed Bigot to the restaurant. There he seemed to be well known. The proprietor himself took charge of them and prompted their decision on the important subject of the wines appropriate to the solids. They "did themselves well." Their conversation covered subjects far more interesting to them than the case they had in hand. Bigot described the relations that existed in France between the police and the criminal courts; he deplored the sentimentality of the French jurymen and the notorious inadequacy of sentences.

"Like you in England we catch our murderers; we provide the evidence sufficient to convict them and bring them to the guillotine, and then the tears begin to flow. The guilty man is the father of a family; the jurymen and the judge too are fathers of families. To commit a little murder in a fit of passion? Why, it is a thing that any of them might do. Let us give the man another chance. A short term of imprisonment will give him time for repentance; he may still become a worthy citizen. In England, I understand, you execute your murderers."

"Some of them," admitted Cooper.

"Well, in France it has become the exception. We have forgotten how to punish, and the public sympathy is always on the side of the gangster."

They discussed the dangers to which French police officers are subject. Bigot was astonished to learn that it was the exception for British criminals to carry pistols. "Here in France it is not only the pistol, but also the knife, and especially is this so with the Italians and the Poles, who furnish the greater part of our criminals. We have officers wounded every year; it is a dangerous profession, that of the police."

When they had well fed and had drunk their coffee and their *petit verre*, Bigot looked at his watch and Richardson called for the bill, which proved not to be as extravagant as he had expected.

"Now, messieurs," said Bigot, "I will take you to the flat where the murder took place. It is quite near. We can go to it on foot."

The *concierge* appeared glad to see the police. "When shall I be able to clean the flat on the second floor, monsieur?" she asked. "The carpet will have to go to the cleaners."

"All in good time, madame," replied Bigot. "If you will now lend me your key, it may bring the moment for cleaning one day earlier. These gentlemen have to visit the flat."

The English detectives found the little sitting-room very much as it must have appeared on the morning after the murder. A stiff brown stain on the carpet indicated the spot where the body had been found. Bigot explained that the only change had been that the chairs had been pushed back to make room for the stretcher, and that a few things had been taken down to the police station. The lamp was still lying on the floor. One overturned chair had been left as it was. Richardson pounced on the waste-paper-basket, half concealed by the window curtain. There was torn paper in it. He pulled a large official envelope out of his pocket and poured into it the tiny fragments of paper, sealing down the flap and labelling it, "Contents of W.P. basket." Then he proceeded to scrutinize every square inch of the floor by the light of an electric torch. Bigot sat down on the divan and watched him with a smile. Cooper, meanwhile, was making a rapid sketch plan of the room, aided by a pocket tape-measure. The room was only twelve feet by fourteen and it was overcrowded with furniture.

Having completed his survey of the carpet, Richardson brought forward a chair, and addressing Bigot, said, "I must ask you to move from the divan, monsieur. If you will kindly take this chair..."

Bigot complied with a laugh. "You English detectives take nothing for granted, I observe."

At a sign from Richardson, Cooper took one end of the divan while Richardson took the other. They brought it eighteen inches forward and tilted it. The carpet under the divan seemed not to have been dusted for many weeks, but the object that riveted the attention of the three men was an exposed roll of film from a Kodak camera. It was lying a few inches in from the edge of the divan.

"Here is something," remarked Richardson.

"You think so? To me it seems quite unimportant. All journalists nowadays carry cameras."

"Where is Mr. Everett's camera?"

"Here," said Cooper, "here on this shelf."

"Let's have a look at it." Richardson took it out of its leather case and measured the exposed film against it. He turned to Bigot. "You see, monsieur? This film could never have been used in this camera; it is two sizes larger."

"*Tiens!*" exclaimed Bigot, "but that is certainly a point; the film may have rolled out of the murderer's pocket during the struggle. We will have it developed."

Richardson had moved over to a little buffet with a marble top. "This room smells strongly of whisky, and now I see why," he said. He pointed to an uncorked decanter, from which a liberal libation had been poured into a glass. A siphon was standing beside it. "Look here, Cooper, this shows that Everett was pouring out a drink either for himself or for a visitor... and... stoop your head a little... he must have seen something in that mirror that made him forget to put the stopper back in the decanter. From where I am standing I can see everything in the room, with the inspector in the centre of the picture. Perhaps it was this fact that led to the fatal quarrel. Well, we'll remember that, but for the moment we have our hands full; we ought to get back and piece these fragments of paper together."

They walked back to the police station, making a little detour to pass a photographer's shop, where Bigot left the film to be developed. Back at their table the two British detectives engaged in the familiar and fascinating game of re-constructing a document out of torn paper. The trick consists, of course, in getting all the outside borders into their proper positions; that gives the size of the sheet, and the rest of the work becomes comparatively easy. It was obvious that the torn-up scraps had belonged to the same document; there were no odd scraps in the basket.

"Hallo!" exclaimed Cooper. "Here's an address."

"An address is always something."

"Yes, but look, this address is embossed—*Cercle Interallié*, Faubourg St. Honoré. I know the place; it's a club, almost next door to the British Embassy; but, as you see, the document itself is written in French."

"Let's get on with our piecing, and then we shall know what the document was."

They went on working at their game for another half-hour before Cooper found himself in a position to read the document aloud. It consisted of note of a story compromising to a member of the French Cabinet at the time.

"I wonder whether a French police station runs to a pot of paste," said Richardson. "This document is written on one side only, so we can paste it down on ordinary thick paper, and not on transparent flimsy as we have sometimes to do at home. See whether you can rout out Bigot and scare a pot of paste out of him."

Two minutes later Cooper returned, carrying a paste-pot in triumph. Paste appeared to be a commodity very largely used by French officials.

"We must get on with our pasting," he said, "or we shall have the inspector on our backs. He wants to see the result of our piecing game."

Actually the inspector followed close upon Cooper's heels, and was able to watch the re-construction of the document with the paste-pot.

"It is in French," he exclaimed with relief. "Then I shall be able to read it. Do you think it has anything to do with the letter signed 'P.C'?"

"Yes, monsieur; it has, in our opinion, everything to do with it. 'P.C.,' whoever he may have been, must have met Mr. Everett at the club, where every member of the British Embassy staff is an honorary member, and 'P.C.' wrote out the story then and there for the information of the British ambassador. Then, for some reason, 'P.C.' must have changed his mind and insisted upon the destruction of the note in his presence. That is how we interpret the two documents. The date can be fixed only by going to the club, where the names of all guests of members are recorded."

A taxi set down the party at the gate of the courtyard, and Cooper suggested that Bigot should enter the club alone; three men interviewing the porter simultaneously might attract too much attention, whereas one would attract none. Bigot acquiescing, the two Englishmen walked towards the British Embassy to see how Mr. Gregory was disposing of his reporters. The tide was on the wane, for the little crowd at the gate in the morning had dwindled to a single photographer, who might be bent upon securing portraits of the two foreigners who had been seen to go in, but not to come out again. They retraced their steps to the club. Bigot emerged triumphant. He had found in the visitors' book the name of Frank Everett, and Paul Chabrol as his luncheon guest, and this had been on Monday, the first of October. All that now remained was to find M. Paul Chabrol and hear what he had to say.

"That will be my task," said Bigot. "Also I shall call for those photographs that we left to be developed this morning; they may yield some light on this mysterious affair."

"Now that we are so near the Embassy," said Richardson, "I think we ought to report our day's work to the first secretary, Mr. Carruthers, I think his name was."

The porter touched his hat as they went in; they were now members of the Embassy staff. The Press photographer had deserted his post, weary of waiting for what seemed never destined to materialize.

Chubb met the two detectives at the door of the Chancery. "They've been asking where you two gentlemen were, and I could tell them nothing. I said that probably you were going over the floor of Mr. Everett's flat with a high-power microscope—that's what they do in the detective films. Number One holds up a hair found on the carpet. 'What's this?' he asks, and Number Two says, 'I know it; it belonged to the beard of the *sous-prefet* who was done to death last Thursday,' and there you are!"

"Are they fond of detective films over here?" asked Cooper.

"They eat them, but always there's a woman in the case— she's the vamp that lured the poor man to his death. When she's off stage they talk about her as the most beautiful woman that you've ever seen, and when you do see her—my God!"

Richardson laughed. "I suppose the canons of female beauty vary for every country. In England the type looks half-starved; here in France it's the other way about; they run to busts. Is the first secretary disengaged?"

"Mr. Carruthers? Oh, he's always busy, you know, but he asked me just now whether you had come in. Stop here and I'll see how the land lies."

Chubb opened a door, looked in, and beckoned to Richardson; the two detectives entered the room.

Carruthers' first question was, "Well, how did you get on with the French police?"

"Very well indeed, sir. They showed us every-thing—the room where the body was found, every-thing that had been taken to the police station, and a mass of documents, mostly in English, which we had to go through."

"Did you find anything that threw a light on the mystery?"

"We found material for further investigation, but it did not amount to very much. In the waste-paper-basket there were a number of scraps of torn paper. We pieced them together and showed them to Inspector Bigot. It was a libellous statement about one of the Ministers, written on club paper, apparently by a guest who was lunching with Mr. Everett the day before the murder. Among the papers that had been brought down to the police station was a letter signed 'P.C.' We have provisionally identified the writer as a certain Paul Chabrol."

"Paul Chabrol? Why, he's a very well-known journalist who signs his articles. What was in the letter?"

"It was written in a peremptory tone, calling upon Mr. Everett to destroy the note in the writer's presence, and saying that he would call at Mr. Everett's flat that evening to see it done."

"I wonder why."

"No reason was given except that the story wasn't true. Probably Paul Chabrol gave his reason to Mr. Everett when he called."

"Doesn't it strike you as rather suspicious that Chabrol hasn't been round to the police to tell them at what hour he called at the flat?"

"Yes, sir, especially if he had an innocent explanation to give."

"Was that all you found?"

"No. sir; we found something else; an un-developed Kodak film which may have dropped out of the murderer's pocket during the struggle."

"Or out of Everett's pocket. I know he had a camera."

"Yes, sir, we found the camera, but this film was two sizes too large for that make."

"You're having the film developed, of course?"

"Yes, sir; M. Bigot is having that done."

"I shall be interested to hear the result."

"I forgot to say that we've been round to the *Cercle Interallié*, because the address of that club was on the torn-up paper. We found that M. Paul Chabrol had lunched there with Mr. Everett on the day before the murder. Bigot is going to interrogate him."

"H'm. We don't seem to have got very far, do we? Did you find nothing else suggestive among Everett's papers?"

"No, sir—in that sense we've had a barren after-noon, unless the Chabrol incident develops. In these cases one can never tell what is going to turn into a clue. Generally, there is something to establish a motive for the crime; here, so far, there is nothing, but I don't despair. Luck so often plays into one's hands. M. Bigot seemed very much pleased with our find in the waste-paper-basket and with our discovery of the film, but personally I saw nothing in the note or in the torn-up paper to cause a quarrel which was to end in a murder."

Chapter Five

WHEN INSPECTOR Richardson and Sergeant Cooper reached the police station the next morning, Inspector Bigot was waiting for them. He beckoned them into his office.

"You are just in time, gentlemen. In the waiting-room opposite is M. Paul Chabrol, and I would like you to hear his answers to my questions."

Richardson was quick to see that their friend Bigot prided himself on his skill in examining suspects. It was a very harmless form of vanity, but it might be difficult afterwards to find words for the expected commendation.

Bigot tapped twice on the floor with his heel; the door was thrown open by a constable, and a tall, thin man with sandy hair and moustache was introduced. The constable left the room, shutting the door behind him.

"Have I the honour of speaking to M. Paul Chabrol?" asked Bigot, who had placed his British colleagues on chairs beside him.

"That is my name," replied the man.

"You are a journalist, I think? You will excuse my ignorance if I ask you for what papers you write?"

"I am special correspondent for a number of provincial papers such as the *Courrier du Midi*, the *Quotidien de Lille*, and a number of others."

"On what subjects do you write?"

"On political gossip very often; sometimes on financial questions—it all depends."

"You know, of course, that the English Press attaché, M. Everett, has met with a violent death."

"Yes, I have read of this in the newspapers."

"You lunched with him at the *Cercle Interallié* on Monday, did you not?"

"I did."

"And then you wrote to him on Tuesday, asking him to destroy what you had written, and saying that you would visit him on that evening to see that the note *was* destroyed?"

"That is so."

"And you did visit him?"

"Yes, at about half-past nine."

Richardson was watching the man's face while he was being questioned; he could detect no sign of embarrassment or hesitation. The replies seemed to be perfectly frank and open. Cooper, who among his other accomplishments had acquired some practice in shorthand, was taking notes of the interview in English.

"Will you tell me what passed at this interview?" asked Bigot.

"M. Everett was expecting me. He received me in the most friendly manner, and invited me to accept a *consommation* with him. This courtesy I declined. I had a special reason for insisting upon the destruction of the note I had given him during the luncheon of the day before. I gave him the reason quite frankly, and he took the note out of his pocket-book, tore it up in my presence, and threw the pieces into his waste-paper-basket. I was in haste that evening, having occasion to telephone to the editor of one of my journals, and so I left M. Everett within a few minutes."

"May I ask the reason for desiring him to destroy that note?"

"The reason was purely a private one. The information I had given to Mr. Everett had been furnished by a confrère who had not told me the truth. He had given me much trouble in getting paragraphs that I had sent to my newspapers cancelled just before they went to press. That is a risk that every journalist has to run."

"Quite so. No one questions your good faith in getting the paragraphs cancelled. It is to be regretted that all journalists do not exercise the same discretion. You parted with M. Everett on friendly terms?"

"Perfectly friendly. You have not asked me what was in the note that M. Everett destroyed."

Bigot smiled. "I did not ask you that because we have the note itself." He pulled from a drawer the sheet which Richardson and Cooper had laboriously reconstructed.

"Ha, ha! You took these fragments from the waste-paper-basket in Everett's apartment?"

"We did. How long had you known M. Everett?"

"Only ten days or so. I was told that he was attached to the British Embassy in connection with Press matters and I, who am interested in public affairs in England, got a French colleague to present me to him. The invitation to lunch at the *Cercle Interallié* last Monday followed that introduction."

"The tone of your note to him, written on Tuesday morning, seemed rather peremptory."

"Do you think so? You must make allowance for a journalist who is overworked and who was smarting under the disagreeable discovery that a man whom he trusted had deceived him. At any rate Mr. Everett bore me no malice. Did you invite me down here because you suspected me of being guilty of an assassination?"

"I invited you here as I have invited others who visited M. Everett's flat on Tuesday, to give an account of the reason for the visit. As a journalist you will recognize that that is the first duty of a police officer who is charged with the inquiry into a death."

Chabrol smiled a little sarcastically. "And if their answers do not satisfy you, further steps are taken?"

"Sometimes. I confess to some surprise that when you read of the tragedy in the rue St. Georges you did not at once come to us to give the explanation you have just made."

"I did not think that was necessary. I was not the last person who saw M. Everett that evening. While I was actually saying good-bye to him on the landing a colleague, M. Pinet, who writes for the *Crédit National*, arrived on the landing and was shaking hands with M. Everett as I went down the stairs. Probably others visited the apartment at a later hour."

Both Richardson and Cooper were astonished at the next question put by their French colleague. "Have you ever visited the *Jardin Zoologique* in the Bois de Vincennes?"

Chabrol seemed to be equally surprised by the question.

"Yes, in common with all other Parisian journalists, I suppose, I have visited them."

"Did you take your camera with you?"

"No, monsieur, for the excellent reason that I do not possess one. The articles I write are never illustrated."

"Did any of your journalist friends ask you to get a film developed for them?"

"No, monsieur. I am curious to know the reason for these last questions."

Bigot smiled enigmatically. "If you follow the case, monsieur, I have no doubt that your curiosity will be satisfied. I am much obliged to you for coming here and I will not detain you any longer."

The formal leave-taking between the two was of the usual impressive kind. Bigot went so far as to open the door for his departing guest. He was smiling as he returned to his writing-table.

"No doubt you have guessed why I put those questions about the photographs? I have the developed films found in Mr. Everett's flat in this drawer; they are a disappointment. There are eight of them—all pictures of animals in their enclosures in the Zoological Gardens at Vincennes."

"Is there no photograph of a person?" asked Cooper.

"Not one. You can see them if you like."

"We will take your word for it, M. Bigot," replied Richardson.

"What do you think of M. Chabrol?"

"We both thought that he was telling the truth, monsieur, and we were greatly struck with the skill which you showed in questioning him."

Bigot purred with satisfaction. "It is the result of long practice combined with a knowledge of human nature. Without that I should be lost. It will be useful to you to have seen how we manage these things in France. I have another witness to interrogate. She ought to be here in a few minutes. I think that you should be present while I question her."

"Who is the lady?"

"Madame Blanchard—the lady whom the news-papers call Mademoiselle X."

He opened the door and crossed the passage to the waiting-room. "This way, madame," the detectives heard him say with a great show of gallantry. He ushered into the room a young woman of striking beauty—of beauty rendered even more striking by the marks of sorrow in her features.

"Take this seat, madame," said Bigot, bringing the chair a little nearer to the table. "I want to ask you a few questions in the presence of these gentlemen."

The lady glanced at Richardson inquiringly.

"Who are these gentlemen?" she asked.

"Police officers like myself. You can talk quite openly before them without any fear that what you say will find its way into a newspaper."

She seemed relieved and turned to Bigot, who began his examination.

"Your name is Elise Blanchard, the wife of M. Edouard Blanchard, a civil servant at present in Algiers. You are living with your parents at 8 rue Chaptal. How long have you been married?"

"We married two years ago."

"Any children?"

"No, monsieur."

"There has been no question between your husband and yourself about a separation?"

The young woman flushed, but she replied quite calmly, "No, monsieur."

"How long have you known Mr. Everett?"

"I met him for the first time about three months ago. He was presented to me by a journalist friend. He made himself very agreeable."

"And you became attached to one another?"

She flushed again. "We became attached, yes, but our friendship was quite honourable, on his side as well as mine."

"Did he know that you were married?"

"Not, I think, until about ten days ago, or perhaps it was less. I did wrong in not telling him earlier; I see that now, but you must understand my fear that if I told him he would see me no more. He was not like a Frenchman in those matters, but when he asked me to marry him, of course I had to tell him."

"The news of his death was a great shock to you, madame?"

Her eyes filled with tears and she stifled a sob; not being able to trust her voice she bowed her head in acquiescence. Mastering her voice at last, she asked, "Tell me, monsieur. Is it possible that he killed himself after learning that I was married? The thought of that haunts me day and night."

"Then let me remove that fear, madame. The doctors are in agreement that he met his death at the hands of an assassin, and that he could not have killed himself."

"Thank God for that, but who could have killed him?"

"I was going to ask you if he had any enemy?"

A look of terror came into her eyes. "He told me once that he had one enemy—a deputy, who afterwards became a Minister. The quarrel arose out of quite a trifling incident. Shall I tell you?"

"Please do."

"You must know that M. Everett went out to the Place de la Concorde on February 6th, and was present when the *Garde Republicaine* fired on the demonstrators. He told me that he was only there as a private observer to see all that passed, and he was quite close to the bridge when the order was given to fire and men were shot down; that a deputy who was one of the Ministers at the time made his escape from the Chamber in an omnibus. He was recognized by the crowd, and when the omnibus stopped in a traffic block in the rue Royale, they tried to drag him out of the vehicle with the intention of lynching him, but he took refuge in a café. Mr. Everett told this story to a journalist friend, who published it without Mr. Everett's permission."

"I remember reading the story in one of the newspapers, madame," said Bigot. "Did the deputy in question get to know from whom it came?"

"Yes, monsieur. The deputy found out from the newspaper office the name of the correspondent who had supplied the paragraph, and he sent a friend to tax him with it. The gentleman replied that he had reported only what Mr. Everett had told him, and that Mr. Everett had said that he had witnessed the incident. Thereupon the deputy sent his seconds to Mr. Everett to challenge him to a duel, and Mr. Everett laughed at them and said that Englishmen did not fight duels, but if the gentleman still felt aggrieved he was quite ready to meet him with his fists. This infuriated the deputy, who could not bear to be laughed at. Ever since that day he has been Mr. Everett's enemy—indeed he tried to move the Quai d'Orsay to tell the British Foreign Office that he was a *persona non grata* (is that how you say it?), but the Quai d'Orsay told him that this was impossible."

"And the name of the deputy?"

"Must I say the name?"

"I fear that you must, but your name will not be divulged. You need have no fear on that score."

"It was M. Quesnay, the deputy for the Bouches du Rhône."

"I remember now that that was the name given, madame. And M. Everett did not tell you of any other enemy?"

The young woman shook her head. "Mr. Everett was not a man to make enemies. He was a lover of France, and made friends, but never enemies."

"Have you written to your husband to tell him what has happened?"

It was an unwelcome question, as Richardson divined from the expression on her face when she thought of her husband.

"No, monsieur," she said at last; "he will hear of it quite soon enough when the newspapers discover me. I do beg of you not to betray me."

"Have no fear of that, madame. But had you not better quit Paris until this affair is forgotten?"

"I have nowhere else to go, monsieur. My parents live in Paris. They can spare no money for me to go into the country. I am living with them now."

Bigot swung round in his chair to whisper to Richardson, "Have you any question you would like to ask her?"

Richardson shook his head. "You have her address, monsieur. If anything fresh comes to light you can always send for her again."

"Good. Madame, I will not detain you any longer. Go home to your parents and try to forget what the newspapers say about you."

The young woman rose, bowed comprehensively to her three interrogators, and left the room.

Bigot beamed on his English colleagues as who should say, "I did that rather well, don't you think?"

Richardson could do no less than congratulate him on eliciting the story of the deputy who had so narrowly escaped the lamp-post on February 6th. "He certainly must have been an enemy of Mr. Everett's."

"Yes, my friend; a very bitter enemy, because no deputy can afford to become a laughing-stock, and for Mr. Everett to laugh when challenged to a duel was a deadly insult."

"You will invite this M. Quesnay to an interview?" asked Richardson, not knowing how far the powers of a police superintendent extended.

"Interrogate a deputy who has now become a Minister?" exclaimed Bigot, his eyebrows rising to meet his hair. "He would not come. He would go and complain to the *Prefet*, and I should be called to account. A Minister? No!"

"Will that young lady's name get into the news-papers? I should be sorry if it did."

"If she's prudent and abstains from running about to cafés, she'll be safe enough from the Press in Paris. So far, all that the reporters know is that a certain unmarried lady, whom they call 'Mademoiselle X,' was in some mysterious way mixed up with the case. They do not know her name or where she lives, nor do they know that she has a husband. That does not mean that her photograph will not appear in the newspapers."

"Her photograph?" exclaimed Richardson. "If they have her photograph..."

Bigot laughed at this innocence. "It will not be the photograph of the lady who has just left us; it will be that of the best-looking among the young typists in the editor's office, and the account of her and the interview with her will be written by one of these newspaper gentlemen. It will not lack sensation, I can promise you."

"Oh, is that the way it's done?"

"Don't they do that in your country—the newspapers?"

"No, they would be afraid of being exposed by rival editors."

"Ah! Here in Paris they are safe, because they all do it. The feeling of a rival newspaper would be regret that they hadn't got in first with a better-looking girl. The girls themselves enjoy seeing their photographs in the newspapers, and a little *douceur* in good French money keeps their mouths shut. I haven't asked you what you thought of the young lady?"

"We thought that she was telling the truth."

"You were right. She was telling us the exact truth, for it coincided with much that I already knew. It does not help us very far in pinning the crime to a particular person, but it does supply a motive."

Cooper ventured to intervene. "It need not have been the deputy himself; one of his seconds might have felt insulted."

"Quite so. Fortunately I have means for obtaining precisions in the lives of deputies, and I shall avail myself of these." It was evident that he was still athirst for praise. "You did not think that I pressed the lady unduly hard?"

"On the contrary, M. Bigot, we both thought that your restraint and tact were admirable."

"You haven't yet heard me examining a rascal with a dozen convictions to his account. Ah! Then it is another affair. I take off my gloves and let my claws peep out. It may take time to obtain a confession, but in the end I succeed. You may ask any of the habitual criminals, and you will hear that Bigot of the ninth *arrondissement* is a man to keep clear of. And now, messieurs, you must be as hungry as I am. Let us adjourn for lunch, and when you come back I will send one of my men with you on the trail of M. Pinet."

Chapter Six

WHEN RICHARDSON and his companion returned to the office they learned from the doorkeeper that M. Bigot had gone out and it was not known when he would return. "I believe that M. Verneuil is to put himself at your disposal. I will call him."

Charles Verneuil, as the British detectives came to know later, had been a petty officer in the French navy. He was a man on the wrong side of forty, with a rather rolling gait when he walked, and a broad chest. He was as little like a detective as it is possible to imagine. His eyes were shrewd and humorous; a sarcastic twist of the lips might convert his humour into winged darts of satire. He greeted his British colleagues warmly, though not without a hint that he expected them to provide him with an afternoon of entertainment. He came from the west of Brittany.

"I have instructions from M. Bigot," he said, "that the first thing to do is to find a M. Pinet, a journalist who writes for the *Crédit National*. With your permission we will go straight to the office of that journal in the rue Réaumur."

They took the Metro. When they reached the modest office of the journal, Verneuil stopped an old acquaintance who came running down the stairs, and asked him whether M. Pinet was in the building.

"No, monsieur; he has been absent for four or five days. He had an accident."

"Then I will write to him if you can give me his address, monsieur."

"*Hélas!* I do not know it. I only know that he has lately changed it." The young man stopped a colleague who was making for the door. "These gentlemen are asking for Richard's address. You who know everything that goes on in the world can tell me."

"Richard is leading a monastic existence at le Pecq, they say."

"Monastic?" queried his friend.

"Monastic as far as his latest platinum blonde will let him, but I cannot give the name of his villa; le Pecq is a small place; any tradesman there could direct you."

That seemed to be sufficient for Verneuil, who hurried his companions back to the Metro and changed at the Opera for St. Lazare. They booked for le Pecq, the last station before St. Germain, and crossed to a garage opposite the station. There M. Richard Pinet appeared to be well known. A garage hand was good enough to come out into the road and point out the Villa Mariette. "You can't miss it," he said; "the name is on the gate."

The party walked for about three hundred yards along the road to Croissy before they found it. It was a small villa with a neatly clipped hedge that gave privacy to the garden. One had to ring the bell at the gate, which was locked. "Monastic seclusion," observed Verneuil. The bell sent a peal through the house; the front door opened and a lady with platinum blonde hair and painted finger-nails came tripping down the steps in shoes with inordinately high heels.

"You desire, messieurs?"

"We have come to see M. Pinet," explained Verneuil archly; his tone betokened that he had little desire to discuss his business with this charmer who smelt powerfully of scent, and whose daily *toilette* apparently consumed a good deal of the morning.

The lady was not to be put off. "On what business, messieurs?"

"That we shall explain to monsieur in person when we see him."

"M. Pinet can see nobody; he is recovering from a serious accident on his motor-bicycle and his doctor has prescribed complete rest."

"I regret it, madame, but we must see him. We are police officers. If he cannot come down to us, we will go up to his bedroom. Even if it takes him the rest of the afternoon to rise and come down to us, we shall stay here. We can always occupy our leisure time by making a search of the house—the drawers and cupboards—if madame will be so good as to replace everything after we have left." He screwed up one eye with a grin.

"I cannot see by what right you come here to disturb a sick-room; it is scandalous," protested the lady, but Richardson observed that she was backing towards the stairs.

Verneuil took advantage of her retreat to enter the dining-room. His British companions followed him. Verneuil cocked his ear to listen to sounds from above which were brought to them through the ceiling. He held up his finger. They heard the murmur of the platinum blonde and responses in a male voice, then a bump overhead suggested that someone was tumbling out of bed and collecting dressing-gown and slippers. There followed footsteps on the stairs and presently a man in pyjamas, dressing-gown and slippers blocked the doorway.

"To whom have I the honour of speaking?" he said, as the police officers rose from their chairs.

Verneuil took from his pocket-book a card and presented it.

"And these gentlemen?"

"Colleagues of mine. Shall we be seated?" asked Verneuil. "I understand that you are suffering from an accident, and that your doctor has prescribed rest and quiet."

"I say that your intrusion is unwarrantable," began Pinet in a high-pitched voice. "What right have you to force your way into my house when you knew that I was ill in bed?"

Richardson and Cooper were looking keenly at the man, who belonged to a type that they had never met before. He was sallow and thin, about thirty years of age, and looked as if he were on wires; his temperament made him beat down every question with a flood of nervous eloquence. The detectives noticed that Verneuil threw himself back in his chair with an air of resignation whenever the flood-gates were opened; it was useless to try to close them before the waters ceased to gush. Richardson rallied his French colleague about this later in the afternoon. The reply was that Pinet's accent betrayed him as a Bordelais, and you might as well try to stop a thunderstorm as a man from Bordeaux.

Shorn of three-quarters of its verbiage, Pinet's account of his movements on the previous Tuesday evening was as follows. Yes, he had visited the flat of the British attaché that evening by appointment. His editor desired to know how the British equalization fund was being administered, and M. Everett was in a position to enlighten him. He could not remember how long he had known M. Everett—how can a busy journalist remember such data as these when he is seeing different people at every hour of the day? It was not reasonable to expect it. At any rate he had known him for some months and had always found him a charming man, who gave in-formation to his French colleagues frankly and without hesitation or reserve. That was why he applied to him. The hour was late? Not for a journalist, it was barely ten o'clock, and besides, M. Everett could not have received him earlier because he had another visitor, and he was expecting yet another when he (Pinet) had left.

"Was your interview with him a pleasant one?"

"Most pleasant, monsieur. He was a charming host and, if I may mention it, he offered to his French visitors the most delicious whisky to be obtained in Paris. He whispered to his intimates, of whom I was proud to be one, that it came over from London in the diplomatic pouch."

Richardson intervened in his foreign-sounding French which seemed to startle Pinet, who almost bounded in his chair. "Did you drink any whisky with Mr. Everett that evening?"

Pinet emitted a forced laugh. "What a searching question, monsieur! I am one of those wise men who never refuse a tempting offer."

"At what hour did you leave the flat?" asked Verneuil.

"There again you put me in a difficulty, monsieur, for how can anyone speak of the passage of time without looking at his watch. This afternoon, for example, *you* might put the length of our interview at half an hour and I at two hours or three. I think I must have been in Mr. Everett's flat for perhaps half an hour."

"You know, of course, that he was found dead in his flat the next morning?"

"I saw it in the newspapers and you can guess what a shock it was to me."

"You did not stay longer than half an hour, you think?"

"Certainly no longer; perhaps not so long. As a matter of fact M. Everett seemed anxious to be rid of me, though his manners remained perfect. He seemed to be nervous about the visitor he was expecting; seemed constantly to be listening for sounds from the staircase."

"This other visitor did not arrive before you left?"

"No, monsieur; there was no one on the stairs when I went out. Mr. Everett came out on the landing with me to switch on the light, and he begged me to turn it off when I got to the bottom."

"Did he give you any hint about the identity of the visitor he was expecting?"

Pinet reflected with knitted brow. "My first impression was that it might have been a lady, and then another suggestion flashed across my mind...that it was...no, I don't think that I ought to repeat it to you."

Verneuil cocked a humorous eye at him. "Come on; you may as well tell the whole story."

"I don't want to keep anything back, monsieur, but it was only my surmise. I thought that it might be one of M. Quesnay's seconds who was calling upon him again to get him to write an apology to his principal. Every journalist knows that M. Quesnay will not let the matter drop until he has obtained satisfaction."

Verneuil seemed puzzled. "Satisfaction for what?"

"Ah! I thought that everybody in Paris knew that story. M. Everett had told a journalist that M. Quesnay had escaped from the Chamber during the disturbances on February 6th and had boarded an omnibus; that the crowd in the rue Royale recognized him and tried to drag him out of it, but that he took refuge in a café and hid himself in a lavatory. M. Quesnay declared the story to be a lie, and sent his seconds to challenge M. Everett to a duel. Monsieur repulsed them with insults."

"Who were M. Quesnay's seconds?"

"That I cannot tell you. I know no details, but I believe the story to be true. I am not suggesting that one of the seconds committed the crime, and I know nothing of what happened in the flat after I left."

"On the way home, we understand, you had an accident?"

"Yes. I had come on my motor-bicycle. You know what the traffic is like at night when you reach the Place de la Concorde—vehicles and lights going at incredible speed in every direction. It was in trying to avoid an automobile coming across the Place from the Champs-Élysées that I struck the kerbstone and was flung forward against a lamp standard. I was dazed, my arm and hand were bruised and bleeding; my motor-cycle was badly damaged. If a bystander had not come to my aid I might have lain there all night. No, monsieur, it is very unsafe to ride through Paris on a motor-cycle after dark."

"Did you bleed much?" asked Verneuil.

"I cannot tell you that, monsieur; I was too much dazed to see."

"What happened to you then?"

"One of your *agents* came up and telephoned for an ambulance, which took me to the Hospital Beaujon. He told me not to be anxious about my motor-cycle; that it would be taken to a garage for repair. Well then, there I was. They dressed my arm in the accident ward and put me into a taxi for St. Lazare, and I was fortunate in finding another taxi at le Pecq station; it was a costly journey."

Sergeant Cooper had been busy taking notes. He asked for the address of the hospital and learned that it was in the Faubourg St. Honoré. There were several points in the man's narrative that required checking. There was a long pause; Verneuil appeared to be reflecting.

"May we see the shirt and coat you were wearing?"

"Alas, monsieur, both have been washed.

"The name and address of your doctor, monsieur?

"Dr. Monier; 17 rue d'Ourches, St. Germain."

"When does he think you will be fit to go to Paris again?"

"He did not say."

"Have you a camera, monsieur?"

"I have. Do you wish to see it?"

He rose painfully to his feet and whispered to the platinum blonde lady who appeared to be lurking in the passage outside. She was heard struggling with something heavy under the staircase and presently appeared with an imposing studio camera of large dimensions.

"Is that your only camera?" asked Richardson. "Have you no portable camera like other journalists?"

"No, monsieur. I practise photographs as an artistic hobby—not for news purposes."

Verneuil became restless. He rose heavily from his chair, closed his note-book slowly as if he was cudgelling his brains to suggest any other questions. "Well, monsieur," he said at last, "those are all the queries I shall put to you to-day. You had better get back to bed as soon as you can."

Followed by his two companions he made for the door, scaring away the platinum blonde, who seemed to have had her ear at the keyhole. With a curt "*Au revoir*, madame," he passed out of the house.

"Where are we going now, monsieur?"

"To St. Germain to call on Dr. Monier. We'll check that fellow's statement as we go. The doctor may have something useful to tell us; an alleged accident might be a good cover for wounds received in a fight; one never knows."

"You don't think he was telling the truth, then?" interposed Cooper.

"Bah! How many men in this world tell the truth when they are questioned by police officers, or for the matter of that, when they are telling a story to their friends. To most men the gift of speech was intended by Providence for concealing the truth. Ah!

I forgot that you had had the privilege of hearing M. Bigot in one of his famous interrogations. First the sugar, then the butter, and then the mustard and vinegar. You must have observed his method, but even he, though he doesn't know it, fails to arrive at the truth."

"What did you think about that story of the seconds of M. Quesnay challenging Everett to a duel?" asked Richardson.

"Reporters' guff, I should say."

"Yet M. Bigot was told the same story by the young woman with whom Mr. Everett was consorting. She had heard it, she said, from Everett himself."

Verneuil checked his walk to look quizzically at Richardson. "It may be true. The follies of politicians are past wondering at, and their feuds are past counting."

"Is M. Quesnay an important person in the Chamber?" asked Richardson innocently.

"Have you ever heard of a French politician who is important?"

"But he was a Minister."

Verneuil spat eloquently, but made no other reply.

They found the rue d'Ourches without difficulty, but the doctor was engaged, and four or five people of the humbler class were waiting to see him. It was a case for the use of the official card, and the poor patient—a woman who intended to have her money's worth with the aid of her tongue—was hustled out of the consulting-room to make room for the distinguished visitors. The doctor was a bearded man with ascetic features. His clothing showed that he was having a struggle to make both ends meet. On hearing that these three healthy-looking police officers were not patients, but had come to waste his time, he bristled.

"M. Pinet? Yes, he is one of my patients." He pulled out a well-thumbed pocket-book. "Yes; he had an accident. He told me that he had fallen off his motor-bicycle and his arm had bled profusely. It could not have been a very serious affair, for I see that he had only superficial bruises and grazes to the skin. These I dressed on Wednesday last."

"You paid him other professional visits, I think?"

"Other visits? Then I must have visited him in my sleep. This note-book tells me that I saw him once only, and that was last Wednesday."

"You did not see him yesterday or the day before?"

"No, monsieur, but if he asserts that I did I shall be very glad to charge him for the visits." A wan smile dawned in his face. He became confidential. "These gentlemen from Paris who take villas in Croissy and le Pecq to entertain their ladies and wish to enjoy short holidays are very apt to send for us to certify that they are ill and unfit to attend their offices. You need have no anxiety about M. Pinet. If I visit him again it will be to recommend a little gentle exercise in the streets of Paris after office hours."

"That seems to be all that we can do this afternoon, M. Verneuil," observed Richardson when the door had closed behind them.

"Yes, that is all. Pinet was lying, but that does not prove him to have been guilty of a crime. There was no motive as far as I can see, whereas with that attractive blonde lady in the house, he might well have had a motive for taking a few days' holiday. If we were to visit the house-agents probably we should find that he had taken the villa furnished for a month and had paid the rent in advance. That is a common practice with these young fellows."

As they walked to the station Richardson said, "I suppose you will get Pinet's account of his accident verified by the constable who was on duty that night in the Place de la Concorde?"

Verneuil laughed sarcastically. "Oh, you English police—you're all alike. You take nothing for granted. Everything has to be cleared up to the smallest detail as you go. Assuredly I shall verify the accident by inquiring at the eighth *arrondissement*, and you'll see it will be a sheer waste of time. The man did have an accident, and made the most of it for reasons not unconnected with that platinum blonde of his. I suppose in London it takes you months to clear up the simplest case."

Richardson laughed. "We never look on verifying work as waste of time, M. Verneuil."

The rattle of the electric train and the crowded car made conversation impossible on the return journey. Verneuil composed himself to sleep with his mouth open, and snored so loudly that the woman beside him changed her seat at the next stop. At St. Lazare the Englishmen shook hands with their French colleague, promising to meet him on the morrow.

As the two C.I.D. officers walked back to their hotel, they discussed their afternoon's work.

"So far," said Cooper, "we don't seem to have discovered anything material. I didn't like that fellow Pinet, but his story seemed to hang together. He lied, of course, about the gravity of his accident, but he may have had some other reason for that."

"What I was looking for was the motive, and I'll be hanged if I can see one. The man who might have had a motive was that Deputy Quesnay, or one of those seconds of his. The crime had all the appearance of a fight, in which the man who was getting the worst of it used a knife. But there was one lie Pinet told us that could be disproved at once. You remember him saying that he drank a glass of whisky with Everett. No one drank whisky in the flat that night; whisky had been poured into the glass, it is true, but the other glass on the sideboard was clean, and I took the trouble to look round the two rooms for a dirty glass. There was no other, dirty or clean, and the glass with the whisky in it had not been touched. Anyhow, when we've had a bite of supper we'll go in and write up our report; it helps to clear one's mind."

Chapter Seven

SITTING OVER their breakfast next morning—a breakfast in which bacon and eggs played their part—the two detectives discussed their future plans.

"If we don't report progress to the Embassy," said Richardson, "there'll be trouble, and as we seem to have nothing to do this morning, we'll take it easy till ten o'clock and then go down to Mr. Gregory. We ought to find out whether he knew of this challenge to a duel."

"Yes," said Cooper, "but it's Sunday."

"Yes, I know, but when I last saw him, Mr. Gregory said that he would be at the Embassy at ten in the morning."

When they reached the Embassy at that hour they were told that Mr. Gregory had arrived. "Twenty minutes before his usual time," remarked Chubb, "and there's no Sunday for me, either." He escorted them along the passage and announced them.

"Ah! You've turned up at last. Everyone has been running round in circles wondering what had become of you. Have you had any luck?"

"We've made some slight progress, sir, but nothing to write home about. We looked in not so much to report progress as to ask you a question. Did you know that a deputy named Quesnay had challenged Mr. Everett to a duel?"

"Good Lord! Has that page of ancient history been turned up? Everett told me all about it. Quesnay is a poor fish without the guts to do anything drastic. If Everett had accepted the challenge, Quesnay would have insisted on the condition that at the first scratch that produced blood the doctors were to step out and stop the proceedings. That's what duelling has come to in France, but Everett didn't know that to laugh was the direst insult that could be given, and Quesnay has never forgotten it."

The two detectives exchanged glances.

"Oh! If you think you're getting warmer I must undeceive you. Quesnay wouldn't hurt a fly if it would damage his political future. He's a Minister of some kind, and he hopes to get his fingers into the till. A little murder would dish him politically, whereas a duel where he ran into no personal danger would be a good advertisement."

"But mightn't one of his seconds have—"

Gregory laughed. "If French duelling seconds knew that they might be let in for committing a murder, they would all with one accord beg leave to be excused from carrying the challenge. Besides, it would be most damaging to our good Quesnay to see one of his seconds in the dock. No, I'm afraid you must put that duel out of your heads. Have you anything else to report?"

"Well, sir, we've seen Mademoiselle X, as they call her."

"The devil you have! How did you see her?"

"We were present at her interrogation."

"You seem to be getting on with your French colleagues."

"I think M. Bigot rather fancies himself at interrogations, and he wanted us to play the gallery."

"What was she like?"

"A very handsome young woman, sir; quite a lady. We felt very sorry for her, and we hope that no journalist will get hold of her address."

"Have you seen all the people who visited Everett on Tuesday night?"

"We have seen two of them. M. Chabrol came quite well out of the interrogation. He can be dismissed. We are not so sure about the other man, a journalist named Pinet, but there is no real suspicion against him so far. He had no motive. According to Pinet, when he left the flat, Mr. Everett seemed to be expecting a third visitor, but as yet we have no clue to him at all."

"The question of motive is certainly a puzzle; no one can have gone to the flat to steal. Poor Everett had nothing worth stealing; he had barely enough pay to rub along. What are you going to do next?"

"Well, sir, we are going now to see M. Bigot and hear about what he did yesterday afternoon."

"I wish you luck. I've always heard that luck is one of the chief assets of Scotland Yard. I'm sure you deserve it."

"One thing, perhaps, you can tell me, sir," said Richardson. "Do the French police observe Sunday, or do they treat the day like any other?"

"I am not quite sure what they do about Sunday; my impression is that you'll find them all at their posts. There is very little Sabbatarianism in France."

On arriving at the police station, Richardson found that Mr. Gregory had been right. He sent a message to Bigot that they were at his disposition. Bigot answered the message in person. He was swelling with importance.

"I hope you had a useful afternoon yesterday," said Richardson.

"Let me tell you about it, and then you can judge for yourselves. I discovered—no matter how—that M. Quesnay, the deputy who challenged M. Everett to a duel, was at the *Jardin Zoologique* of Vincennes on the Sunday before the murder. He took a party of school-children with him and paid for their tea; that might mean that their fathers would vote for him at the proper time."

"How did you find this out?" asked Cooper.

"Ah!" replied Bigot with a look of ineffable cunning, "I have my methods. A photograph of M. Quesnay and the party of children appeared in the *Echo de la Seine* of last Monday. I went out to Vincennes and found one of the waiters who had served the deputy's party. He assured me that when M. Quesnay handed over his umbrella and waterproof he handed over also a Kodak camera, and said that he had amused himself and the children by taking photographs of the animals."

"Unfortunately we do not know the size of that camera."

"Not positively, but the waiter assured me that it was larger than most cameras which visitors take into the garden. I think there is enough in this to justify us in assuming that the film found in M. Everett's *appartement* fitted that camera."

Richardson and Cooper exchanged a furtive glance, but remained silent for a moment. Richardson was the first to speak. "Do you wish to interrogate M. Quesnay?" he asked.

"I? Interrogate a deputy? Oh, the matter has to be handled far more delicately than that, though the interests of justice might be served better by an interrogation conducted by myself, than they would be by handing the case over to a mere *Juge d'Instruction*. We have not come to that yet. As I say, one must, in the case of deputies, proceed with infinite tact; it is not a matter that can be delegated to a man inexperienced in such business."

"That I understand. You have, no doubt, taken the initial steps?"

Cooper noticed that this pressing of the question by his colleague was not to M. Bigot's taste. He said, "What my colleague means, I think, is that if such an interrogation is contemplated he should be allowed to be present. The interrogation of a deputy by one so skilled as you are would interest us extremely."

Bigot was mollified. "In the first place a French deputy enjoys immunity from interrogation. This immunity would have to be lifted before we could interrogate M. Quesnay, and it would at once become a very serious matter. Would you be allowed in England to interrogate one of your deputies?"

"The system in England is not the same as yours in France. We are not permitted to question persons who may afterwards be charged with a crime without first warning them that what they say may be used against them at their trial."

Bigot looked from one to the other in stark astonishment. "Why then, of course, they answer none of your questions!"

"In theory the police are debarred from putting any questions to them."

"What an extraordinary country! No, messieurs, I fear that if ever I have to interrogate a senator or a deputy I shall have to do it alone. It would cause great comment if it became known that foreign police officers had been called in to help the Paris police. It would imply a lack of confidence... I am sure that you will understand."

"Perfectly, monsieur."

"Of course if you care to inquire from time to time how we are progressing with the case, I shall always be delighted to see you."

"And on our part, if we hear anything at the Embassy or elsewhere that may be useful to you, we shall consider it our duty to bring it to your notice, monsieur. I suppose M. Verneuil has already reported to you what we did yesterday afternoon?"

"Oh, that... yes, he reported it to me, but you need not waste your time over such trifles when we are on the real track." He dismissed Pinet with a sweeping gesture of contempt.

"M. Verneuil undertook to verify Pinet's account of his accident. In order to complete our report to the ambassador, we should very much like to know the result of his inquiries."

"I will send him to you, messieurs, and if we do not meet again for a time, let me assure you that the assistance you have given me is very highly appreciated."

They shook hands cordially; it was a polite dismissal.

The Englishmen had no time to discuss their position, for the approaching footsteps of Verneuil resounded in the passage outside. He greeted them with a whimsical smile as he shook hands with them.

"You want to hear what I did after leaving you yesterday afternoon? Well... I found the *agent* who picked up the pieces of our friend, M. Pinet, in the Place de la Concorde on Tuesday night. That gentleman ought to go far in his profession; he has a fine gift of imagination."

"You mean that there was no accident at all?"

"Oh, yes; there was an accident all right. The *agent* said that the gentleman fell off his *moto* and damaged it; that he was bleeding profusely from the nose."

"You mean that the accident was done on purpose?"

Verneuil shrugged his shoulders. "The *agent* could not say that. He said the man was riding very slowly and very carelessly. He seemed to wobble into the refuge when he had a clear road before him, and when he picked him up he seemed to be dazed. That was why he was taken to the hospital. The *agent* telephoned to a repairing garage and they took the *moto* away and mended it. At the hospital they said that a little sticking-plaster would have sufficed for the wounds. Pinet told them that he thought he must have become faint when riding and that he had no memory of the accident."

"He fainted, eh? Such things have happened, of course. Have you found anything indicating who Mr. Everett's third visitor was that night? You remember that Pinet half suggested that it was one of M. Quesnay's seconds."

Verneuil looked at them quizzically. "I dare say that at a later stage, when my inspector has finished his business with M. Quesnay, we shall have to interview that gentleman's seconds. He chuckled inwardly at his thoughts about those interviews. "Yes, certainly they must be interviewed. I shall volunteer for the duty myself." His big frame shook with merriment.

"Duelling seconds committing a murder to vindicate their honour. *Mon Dieu!*"

"I am sorry to say that we shall be leaving you," said Richardson.

"Leaving us?"

"Yes, we gather that M. Bigot has no further need of our services."

"Always this Bigot!" exclaimed the ex-petty officer, half to himself. "My colleague is aiming high; he's out to hunt deputies. He is riding for a fall, like Pinet. Well, I wish him joy of it. But I shall not say farewell to you, because I foresee that we shall still have work to do together, and that when my inspector has finished his business with M. Quesnay, he will expect us to find the real culprit. So it is not *adieu*, but *au revoir*."

The two English detectives set out to walk home in chastened mood.

"I wonder why Bigot has chucked us," said Cooper. "Did we offend in any way?"

"Perhaps we didn't play up to him enough about this duelling business, but probably the real reason is that he believes in himself and doesn't want anyone else to share the laurels with him. I'm not altogether sorry. There is nothing worse in our job than to be working under a man who is barking up the wrong tree."

"What will the Embassy say? Send us back to the Yard with a bad mark against us? After all, we've come up against a dead wall."

"Yes, and it's at the foot of such dead walls that we detective officers find a friend waiting for us. We haven't met him yet in this case."

"What friend?"

"Why, Sergeant Luck, of course. It's at the dead wall that he comes sidling up with a grin on his face. He may be waiting for us round the corner at this very moment."

Cooper sighed audibly. "Personally I don't see any way out. You'll have to see the first secretary to-morrow and what progress can you report?"

"Cooper, you make me tired. We shall never get anywhere if we get discouraged." They were passing the big hotel at St. Lazare. A crowd filled the chairs set in front of the café. "Here, let's have a drink and talk the matter over."

They found a vacant table near the entrance and ordered mild restoratives. Cooper's choice of beer was overruled in favour of *byrrh-cassis* which he had never tasted. While they were awaiting their drinks, Richardson's eye scanned the crowd on either side of them. Suddenly he stiffened.

"Don't look round just yet. That international crook, Polowski, as he used to call himself, is sitting at the fifth table on your left."

"Polowski?"

"Ah! I remember. You weren't in that case. It was great fun while it lasted. What a lot of funny cases the Russian revolution brought to us."

"Was that the case of the Russian gold? I remember something about it. He was trying to dispose of gold which he said had been fished up out of a lake in Russia, where the owner had dropped it to hide it from the Bolshies."

"Yes, that was the case. Polowski and another crook, a Roumanian, were kept under casual observation by Simpson in Central for a week or two, but you know what it is—people won't come forward to prosecute when they think that they will be laughed at as fools for having been done down, or blamed for dealing in stolen property."

"You mean that the men were dealing in base metal and calling it gold?"

"Yes; the sample they produced was gold right enough, but the stuff they tried to sell afterwards was brass. We were trying to get a deportation order against them when they vanished."

"Left the country?"

"Yes; Simpson's attentions had been too pressing, I suppose. At any rate they crossed the Channel, and their names and descriptions were put on the black list at the ports. I wonder what game they are playing over here."

"Probably the same as they did in London. These fellows don't very often change their methods."

Richardson was plunged in thought. "After all," he said at last, "we've been sacked by our friend, Bigot, and we can't sit twiddling our fingers. We've got the Yard to think of. I'll tell you what, Cooper; we won't lose sight of these fellows. If we can establish the fact that they are playing the same game over here in Paris as they were in London, we'll go to the Sûreté about them and perhaps get them to stir up our friend Bigot, who won't want to fall foul of a body like the Sûreté. What about putting them under very discreet observation? You could do it. All you would have to do would be to house them in their hotel, but don't let them spot you. They may have noticed me. I've a sort of feeling at the back of my mind that we are on the edge of something good. We'll sit here until they move. I'll touch you on the foot when they do, and then you'll take leave of me in the French way—you've seen it—we'll both rise, take off our hats, shake hands formally, grin at one another, and you will follow them up and see where they go. I'll sit tight here and settle up with the waiter. Ah! Polowski is tapping on his glass for the bill."

"Do you recognize the other man?"

"No, I can't put a name to him, but there's something familiar about his face. Ah! There's the waiter. Get ready to bid me *bon appetit* and get on their heels."

They took leave of one another in the real French way and Cooper, who had had years of practice in "shadowing," ran across the studded crossing-place just in time to pick up the trail. The street-lamps were being lighted. Richardson sat on for nearly half an hour, wondering what this chance meeting with Polowski would bring him.

Chapter Eight

POLOWSKI and his unrecognized friend led poor Cooper a dance. It would be impossible to imagine anything more futile than the proceedings of the quarry. They crossed the Boulevard Haussmann and turned into the rue Vignon, which they followed up to the back door of the Café Veil; they pushed through the back door while Cooper strolled round to the front. He knew that he was taking a risk of losing such wary birds, but it would never have done for him to follow them in. His heart gave a bound when he recognized them sitting in the crowded front of the café and giving their order to the waiter. They had passed clean through the building.

The café being a wide one, Cooper was able to pass through another door into the interior and place himself almost behind them with a plate-glass window between. He ordered a drink and kept a wary eye upon their movements. They were deep in conversation; presently they rose to greet a third man, who sat down beside them. Their heads went together; they must have been talking almost in whispers. Cooper beckoned to the waiter and paid his bill, but sat on where he was until his men had also paid for their drinks, when they went off in the direction of the Madeleine. Fortunately for Cooper the Boulevard was crowded with employees going home; he could follow his men without risk. They skirted the Madeleine and walked down the rue Tronchet in the direction of St. Lazare station. Apparently all three were bent upon some quest that they had in common. They climbed the steps to the booking office; went to the window marked first class, and Cooper pressed in behind them near enough to see that Polowski asked for three first-class return tickets to le Pecq. On this he himself took a second-class single for the same place, seated himself in the train, after seeing his quarry enter a first-class compartment, and became busy with his thoughts.

"Return tickets?" he mused. That meant an evening call upon someone in le Pecq. Where were they going to dine? Or were they keeping a dinner appointment in le Pecq? What an extraordinary coincidence that he should have to visit le Pecq twice in two days. Surely this could not be the luck that his colleague Richardson was always counting upon—that this second visit to le Pecq would prove to be connected with the first. That third man? Who was he? A man with a cauliflower ear and a nose a little out of the straight; a man with the powerful torso of a prize-fighter would not be a pleasant guest in any civilized dining-room. They must be going to pay a short evening call. Clearly the little party would be worth following.

Then he turned to the question of how this could be done in the dark. The train was a slow one, stopping at every station to drop passengers who spent their working days in Paris. Most of them would be put down long before le Pecq was reached. He would have to stay in his compartment until his little party had passed the barrier. Would he be able to pick them up again in the dark? Heavens! How this train loitered!

Croissy at last—the next station before le Pecq. At least a hundred people alighted; the train proceeded nearly empty.

But in the light from the platform lamps Cooper had satisfied himself that none of the three men was among them. He moved to the sliding door to get a better view. The train slowed down—the brakes were applied—it pulled up, and was scarcely at rest before three first-class passengers leapt out and were at the barrier with their tickets. They had given no backward glance at the train. But they were out of sight and might have turned either way at the entrance to the station.

Cooper covered the intervening yards quicker than he ever remembered running; describing his gait afterwards, he said that he had taken to wing. Instinctively he avoided the light thrown upon him by the street-lamp and, guided more by sound than sight, he found himself on the track of his men. They were walking three abreast on the narrow road that led past Pinet's little villa. The noise made by their heels on the tarred road made it possible for him to follow them without being overheard.

Cooper checked himself when he judged them to be opposite the little white villa. Would they pass it and so start him off on an inquiry that had nothing to do with the British Embassy, or dared he hope that they would stop at Pinet's gate, ring the bell and summon the platinum blonde? The noise of their heavy boots had ceased. And then, faintly borne to him, came the sound of an electric bell. It was Pinet they had come to see. Cooper did not stop to reflect upon the strange caprices of fortune that had brought this new turn to their affairs just when they had reached the foot of the dead wall. He had to think and think quickly what his next move was to be; it would, of course, be priceless to listen in at the conversations, but they were three to one, and the man with the cauliflower ear and the crooked nose would soon make it clear to him that on Pinet's front door the words "no admittance" ought to be inscribed.

Still, it was a public road; he had as much right to it as they had—he could at least time his passing to the arrival of the platinum blonde at the gate. He went forward. It may be doubted whether any of the three men were aware of him. Out of the corner of his eye he saw the glint of the distant street-lamp on that metallic hair. The lady seemed to be protesting; the gentlemen, or at any rate one of them, to be insisting; voices were raised; the boxer seemed to be advocating a short way with her unless the gate were opened; the others were trying to moderate his tones. Before he passed out of earshot Cooper caught the words, "I tell you, madame, that we *must* see him."

Cooper was now far enough away to make it safe for him to stop, but he heard no more, for the man had overcome the lady's objections, and the gate was shut behind them.

The time of waiting seemed interminable. At last a shaft of light was projected from the front door; the party was coming out. Assuming that they would make for the station, he hung back in the darkness. The only words spoken were "*Au revoir, madame; we shall see you again before long.*" And then the three set out for the station. This time Cooper provided himself with an evening paper and took a first-class ticket to Paris. There being only one first-class coach, he entered it just behind the men, and passed down the corridor to the single seats at the end, where he buried himself behind his newspaper.

The trains make such a noise on the St. Germain line that conversation is impossible except during the brief stops, and even then it was difficult to catch the sense of what they were saying, though he was the only other person in the carriage. One thing was clear; they were not seeing eye to eye. The prizefighter was a man of action, but his plans did not seem to suit the others.

Arrived at Paris, the men took a taxi from the station and drove to a modest hotel just off the rue de Rivoli, followed by Cooper in another taxi, which he stopped at the corner and paid off. Nothing was more natural than for a foreigner visiting Paris to pass the glazed swing-door of the hotel and look in.

Cooper saw the three men make their way to the desk and ask for their keys. He felt that he could now take it for granted that he had reached the end of the long trail. The men were staying at the Hôtel Philippe. There was nothing now to do but find Richardson and report. Cooper found him in his hotel bedroom, writing up his notes.

"You can lay down your pen, inspector, until you've heard what I have to tell you."

Cooper narrated shortly all that had happened during his tour of observation. When he came to the description of the third man who had joined Polowski at the Café Veil, Richardson sat up stiff.

"A thick-set man with a crooked nose and a cauliflower ear, about thirty-five to forty? Was he smoking a pipe?"

"Yes, a rather short pipe. Why, do you know him?"

"From your description I should take him to be Dick Butler, the champion middle-weight, who must have just come out from serving his sentence for blackmail."

"What else has he done?"

"I don't know that he's done anything. Blackmail is his trade and he sticks to it. My old friend Polowski would readily turn his hand to blackmail if he saw a chance of making money out of it. Of course I'll have to see Butler before I can swear to his identity, and that's not going to be easy, because he'd recognize me a hundred yards off."

"There's a little shop next to the hotel—a bookshop. Couldn't you wait just inside and let me give you a signal? We could get along down there at nine o'clock when the shop opens, and then keep observation."

"We will, but that doesn't bring us any nearer to our goal. The murdered man had no money, and therefore if Pinet was guilty he could not have made any money out of the murder.

Why, then, should anyone try to blackmail Pinet? And why should it take three men to do it?"

"Perhaps Polowski was trying on his old wheeze of selling bogus jewellery."

"But why pick out Pinet—a struggling journalist?"

"They might have been trying to get him to write an article for his paper to advertise them, promising to pay him as soon as they got a purchaser," said Cooper.

"H'm! They might. We'll buy a copy of the paper and see, but from what I know of Polowski's methods, I fancy that he would always select some reckless, gambling fellow with money."

"Yes," said Cooper, "but remember that Pinet's paper deals with finance, and this may have become his new way of approach—to boost the gang in an article and then introduce them to the rich dupe. Supposing that you recognize this prize-fighter as Butler, what more can we do? Get him kicked out of France?"

"That must depend upon what Verneuil suggests. My idea is to get Verneuil to work with us now that Bigot has thrown us over."

"Take him entirely into our confidence, you mean?"

"Yes, why not? He doesn't seem to be hand in glove with Bigot, and he'd be rather glad to wipe his eye. Anyhow, we can do nothing further to-night."

At five minutes past nine next morning the manager of the bookshop that abutted on the Hôtel Philippe received a foreign client—a studious-looking young man in horn-rimmed glasses, who asked leave to look over the stock-in-trade before becoming a purchaser. At this early hour the visitor had the shop to himself. He seemed very hard to please and a little absent-minded, for after opening a book and reading a sentence or two, he would gaze out of the window at the passers-by and occasionally move into the doorway, still carrying the book in his hand. This did not alarm the proprietor, since the customer looked honest and had hung up his hat on a peg, from which he could not remove it without being seen. He was very polite, but appeared disinclined for conversation. Once the proprietor did inquire whether he had found anything to his liking, and this produced a sale. He was told to put the book on one side while others were being selected.

The arrival of a fresh customer seemed to disturb the spectacled young man, who retired further into the shop until his departure. It was just after this incident that an eccentric foreigner passed the shop whistling a lively air. The studious young man went swiftly to the doorway and gazed into the street. Not content with this, he snatched his hat from the peg, and murmuring that he must run after a friend who had passed but would return, he made for the rue de Rivoli, where three men from the Hôtel Philippe were just disappearing.

A few minutes later the gentleman returned to complete his purchases. Evidently he had overtaken his friend, for a second foreigner accompanied him. The bill was presented and paid, and the two departed with their parcel.

"You weren't sure at first?" asked Cooper.

"No, because I had only his back view to go by," said Richardson, folding up his shell-rimmed glasses and stowing them in his pocket. "I had to overtake them and get a squint at your prize-fighter from the opposite side of the street. It was Butler all right; I could swear to him anywhere. Prison diet has helped to keep his weight down and cure him of the drink habit. He's looking very fit."

Cooper was thoughtful. "Are you going to the Embassy first to report progress, or to that police station to see Verneuil?"

"We'll dig out Verneuil first. Now that we know that our men are out, Verneuil can question the booking-clerk about them and have a look at their registration forms, but first we'd better have a heart-to-heart talk with him."

It was a curious sensation to return to a police station from which you had been practically dismissed less than twenty-four hours previously. During the walk to the ninth *arrondissement*, Richardson was debating what he would say to Bigot if he encountered him. He could not pretend that he had come to ask for information so soon; he must feign to have important information to give. As a first step he asked to see Commissaire Verneuil, and by a miracle that official was in the police station. He shook hands with the two visitors, almost with a wink suggesting a secret understanding between them.

"Can I have a word with you, M. Verneuil?" asked Richardson. "We have brought you some interesting information."

Verneuil led the way to the room where they had worked on their first day. They were alone there.

"M. Bigot is out, we understand."

The ex-petty officer screwed up his face in a fashion that would have provoked applause in any music-hall. He laid his forefinger against his nose as if commending discretion.

"Yes, he is out. He is consorting with deputies of the Chamber; even now he may be found in the lobby of the senate, trying to get audience with a Minister. He is becoming a great man in these days. Soon we shall see his name and his portrait in a newspaper."

"Then it is quite in order for us to deal with you?"

"And why not? You've dealt with me before. Why not now?"

"It is that we have recognized two, if not three, international criminals who are staying at the Hôtel Philippe."

"Oh, as to that you will find international criminals all over Paris. We French are a hospitable nation."

"Yes, perhaps too hospitable for your interests sometimes, but to resume—last night these men were followed to the house of M. Pinet which we visited with you yesterday afternoon."

"Ha, ha!" exclaimed Verneuil. "This is something new." He fumbled in his pocket for a notebook. "Tell me exactly what happened."

Thereupon Cooper gave him a detailed account of what the reader already knows, and Verneuil began to take a lively interest.

"You have not given me the names of these men at the Hôtel Philippe."

"No, because that would only confuse you. Such men invariably give false names, and if a passport is likely to be required they carry forged ones, but they must have registered at their hotel."

"Good! I shall go down and look at their forms. We can always get such riff-raff expelled from France."

"But do we want that, M. Verneuil? Would it not be better first to find out why they were visiting Pinet?"

"That would entail arresting them and subjecting them to a close interrogation, but with fellows like these, I doubt whether we should get much. So far we have not made progress. Much was hoped from the finger-prints found in the room of the crime. It is a fatality. The only legible prints were those found on a whisky bottle and glass, and these were the prints of the dead man's fingers; all those found in other parts of the room were blurred and unrecognizable. For the moment we won't trouble M. Bigot with this new development. I will visit the hotel this morning, examine their registration forms, and call on you at your hotel later in the day."

"On second thoughts perhaps it would be well to give you the names of two of them; the third man I do not know. The leader of the gang called himself Polowski when he was in London. He was never convicted of fraud because the prosecutors were ashamed to come forward. The prize-fighter went by the name of Richard Butler. He was twice convicted of blackmail, and can only just have come out of prison."

Verneuil screwed up one eye. "You do not seem to have wasted your time, messieurs. Supposing that one of these three men proves to be the third visitor to the flat that night…"

"Or that Butler is blackmailing Pinet."

Chapter Nine

WHEN RICHARDSON and Cooper reached the Embassy a little before midday they found the staff preoccupied. Everett's parents had arrived from London overnight, and Chubb told them that they were closeted with Carruthers, the first secretary.

"The funeral is to be at Père Lachaise this afternoon. I suppose that you'll be going to it?"

"Is everybody attending it?" asked Richardson.

"Yes, everybody except Mr. Dundas. He's got to stop and mind the baby while we're all away. It's to be a quiet affair, but I'll bet that it's leaked out and we shall have a gang of press photographers who'll worry those poor old people to pose for their photographs, and as likely as not take a snap of His Excellency laying his wreath on the grave. I should go if I were in your place. You never know—the murderer may be there to gloat over his handiwork."

"Is Mr. Gregory in?"

"Yes, he's in his room, but you'll find him a bit on the snappy side this morning; as like as not he'll want to know how you're getting on with your job. Come along; I'll announce you."

They hung back in the passage while Chubb went through the formality, and came forward as soon as he beckoned to them. As Chubb had predicted, they found Gregory in a nervous state.

"You've come at a bad moment," he said. "We are all at sixes and sevens with this funeral."

"So we've heard, sir. But we want to have an interview with Mr. Everett's father, and he may be leaving Paris to-night. Besides, if the ambassador doesn't mind, we should like to be present at the ceremony."

"Oh, he won't mind, especially if he knows that you're getting a move on with your investigations. Is it too soon to tell him that?"

"Much too soon, sir. It is impossible to hurry these things, but we hope to have something to tell you when you have more time to hear it. We won't take up any more of your time now."

"Stop a minute. You want to see Everett's father, don't you? I'll tell Chubb to take you to the waiting-room and bring Mr. Everett to you as soon as Mr. Carruthers has done with him."

They had not long to wait; in less than three minutes they heard voices in the passage; the first secretary was taking leave of the bereaved parents. Chubb made his appearance and hissed at them, "You'll have to see them both together. The wife is badly upset and the husband says that he dare not leave her."

"Very well," assented Richardson; "we'll see them both."

It was to be a painful interview and Richardson found himself regretting that he had chosen this particular moment for it. The mother was in tears; her husband had to steer her to the chair which Cooper had placed for her. The father was a tall, spare man in the late fifties, a retired schoolmaster who eked out his savings by occasional excursions into journalism. The dead man had been their only child.

"Sit down here, Mr. Everett," said Richardson, indicating a chair as far away from the mother as he could. "I am an inspector from Scotland Yard; I have come over at the ambassador's request to help the French police in their investigation of the crime. You will be able to help me if you will allow me to put a few questions to you. Had your son any private means beyond his salary?"

"None, except that from time to time—at Christmas and on his birthday—we sent him small presents of money."

"He told you, I suppose, that the cost of living in France was very high?"

"Yes, he did; he sent me once a table of figures showing that it was the dearest country to live in except Russia."

"Why did he enter the diplomatic service?"

"Well, he had always a turn for learning foreign languages, and his French was not as good as his German. He was already a journalist; he had gone through the mill as a reporter on the *Manchester Guardian*, and he thought that if his French was perfect he would have a better chance as a journalist in England later on. I happened to have a friend who was attached to the Foreign Office after the war, and it was through him that I heard of this opening of Press attaché. Of course I'm sorry now that I ever heard of it, and the boy's poor mother will never get over it."

"What we want to get at is a motive for the crime. It couldn't have been robbery because the little money he had in his flat was untouched. Did he mention in any of his letters that he was counting upon getting some special work outside the Embassy?"

"No; he was not a good correspondent—I suppose he was too busy to write letters—but when he did write he seemed to be wrapped up in his work."

"Did he ever mention having trouble with any French people?"

Mr. Everett pondered. "I remember him writing an amusing letter to me saying that a French M.P. had challenged him to fight a duel, but that didn't seem to worry him in any way; he treated it as a comic incident, and said he had offered to fight the gentleman with his fists."

"Did he always write in good spirits?"

"Yes, and from what they tell me here he seemed to have been very popular with the French journalists. Tell me, inspector; have you discovered any clue yet?"

"We are following up certain clues, but it is too early yet to say what they will result in." Richardson glanced at the clock. "I must not keep you a minute longer, Mr. Everett; you have to get your lunch before the funeral, and at the cemetery we shall not have any opportunity of talking. Let me give you one hint that may be useful. The reporters here intend to make the most of this sad business, and they will want to interview you and get Press photographers to take your portraits. You will be perfectly free to refuse, and we shall be quite near at hand to interfere if they annoy you. Your best defence against interviewers is to pretend that you do not understand French; very few of them speak English. Are you going to stay in Paris for long?"

"No, we are crossing by to-night's boat." Richardson shook hands with the poor man sympathetically, bowed to the lady and left the room, taking Cooper with him. On the way out he asked Chubb at what time the party would leave for the cemetery.

"If you're here at two sharp, inspector, and bring a taxi with you, you can follow the Embassy cars, or if you like it better, why not drive out to the entrance to the cemetery, wait for us there and tack on to the procession. We've had a lot of reporters up here this morning, but I didn't give them any dope about the funeral. I expect we shall find them parked outside at Père Lachaise. Anyway, if you'll make straight for me I'll get you passed in."

A funeral in France is one of the dreariest ceremonies that anyone can attend. Five minutes after Richardson's arrival at the gate the ambassador's car hove in sight. Everett's body had been brought into the chapel by the undertaker early in the morning. The Embassy chaplain was in attendance. There were more than twenty reporters and camera-men at the gate. Chubb now became a very active official. No one was allowed to pass in without his *fiat*. Mr. and Mrs. Everett were only just in time; the gates were shut behind them, leaving the reporters and camera men gnashing their teeth.

"They'll get in, you'll see," said Chubb to Richardson; "either they'll bribe this joker here or they'll go round to one of the other gates, which are kept open."

"I don't suppose it matters very much if they do."

"No, except that it will enrage our old man until he's ready to bite any of us. Then he'll go to bed for three days and send for the doctor."

In point of fact Chubb's gloomy prophecy was fulfilled. When the cortege reached the grave-side camera men were streaming up the nearest path, and Chubb could do nothing to stop them. They concentrated upon the ambassador depositing his wreath and upon the father and mother, the chief mourners; but Mr. Everett was quite successful with the reporters after the ceremony. Probably he knew a good deal of French, but he remained gaping and speechless when questions were flung at him.

When the mourners returned to their cars, Ned Gregory fell back to allow Richardson to overtake him.

"How are you going back to Paris?" he asked.

"We'll look for a taxi, sir."

"Lord only knows when you'll find one in this benighted spot; you'd better come in our car; there's room for you both with a squeeze. We'll drive you to the Embassy, and you can then tell us what you've been doing."

It was certainly a squeeze. Maynard and the chaplain, fortunately an attenuated person, with Gregory, were fitted into the back seat; the two detectives sat with their backs to the chauffeur. To judge by the groans emitted by Gregory at the Embassy gate, the unpacking was even more painful than the fitting in.

"Give me a hand, one of you; the Padre's hipbone has made a wound in my side. You'll have to throw all your strength into wrenching me free."

Richardson did what was necessary with a smile, the chaplain remarking, "You know that our friend Mr. Gregory is the chartered jester of the Embassy."

"Now come along, inspector, and make a clean breast of what you've been doing," said Gregory; "probably Mr. Carruthers will want to hear you. I'll ask him."

Carruthers did want to listen, and he joined the party in the attaché's room. Richardson began by narrating their experiences with Bigot which had brought their employment to an end, and then asked Cooper to describe his shadowing of the doubtful characters they had picked up at the café.

"Does this mean that the French police will have nothing further to do with you?" asked Carruthers a little anxiously.

"Not quite that, sir. We are still in close touch with Bigot's second—a M. Verneuil, who does not see eye to eye with his chief. He is making an inquiry for us at the hotel where these swindlers are staying."

"But judging from what you say, the hunting down of these swindlers scarcely seems a matter for the Foreign Office. You are doing it in the interests of Scotland Yard, are you not?" objected Carruthers.

"We cannot yet say, sir. We do not know the object of their visit to Pinet at le Pecq, and, if you remember, Pinet was one of the last persons, if not actually the last, who visited Mr. Everett on the night of the murder. If you will give me another day, or two days, I have a plan that may clear up that side of the case."

"I suppose I mustn't ask you what it is, inspector?"

"I would rather not say until the plan has taken shape, sir, but as soon as it has I shall not fail to take you into my confidence. And now, sir, if you have no instructions to give us, I ought to get back to our hotel. We are expecting a visit from our detective friend, M. Verneuil."

Cooper was silent as they walked back to their hotel.

"What's the matter with you, Cooper? You are very quiet."

"I'm wondering what you are going to do next. You told those gentlemen at the Embassy that you had a plan for dealing with those rascals? It was the first I'd heard of it."

"Quite right. It came into my head as we were driving back from the funeral. Did they ever give you a part in theatricals, Cooper?"

"Only once—when I was in the Police Minstrels, years ago."

"You mean that your performance was so poor that they never employed you again?"

Cooper laughed. "You wouldn't have said so if you had been in the audience. No, it must have been jealousy on the part of the other comics. Why do you ask?"

"Because I've got a part cut and dried for you. Listen. You are a ne'er-do-well spendthrift—that will come easy to you—you look the part."

"Thank you."

"The son of a doting mother who can't refuse you anything. Her dead husband—a West-End jeweller—has left her a considerable fortune. That part of the story doesn't fit you so well or you wouldn't be on the pay-roll of the C.I.D."

"Never mind; I am often throwing money about in my dreams."

"This distressing habit of yours—throwing money about, grossly over-tipping waiters—is observed at a café by Polowski and his friends. You leave the café just a little unsteady on your pins. The next day you are there at the same hour; a fascinating lady strolls in and sits down at a neighbouring table; you ogle her."

"My God! What would my wife say?"

"Nothing, because she won't be there to see."

"But how am I to know what café these blighters frequent? How are we to locate them?"

"We must take our chance. After all, you followed them to the Café Veil last night, and from what I know of these rascals, they use the same place to meet in night after night until they get blown upon. London doesn't suit them as well as Paris in that respect, because they are aiming at higher game than the people who frequent a Lyons' tea-shop or the people who chose the saloon bars in public-houses."

"And if I find them at the Café Veil?"

"Well, then, you have to take a table within view of them and play the part of a reckless young man who flings his money about. The rest will depend upon your skill as an actor."

"But how is all this going to help us to find Everett's murderer?"

"I can't tell you that either. These fellows live by their wits; they've always some scheme on hand for raising the wind, and you have to find out what their present scheme is. If you win their confidence we may get to know why they visited Pinet at le Pecq."

"Perhaps they wanted a newspaper man in their scheme."

"And for that reason one of them may have called on Everett; that prize-fighter chap wouldn't stick at a little thing like murder."

"Oh, I begin to see what you're driving at. You think that one or other of the gang will sidle up to me and strike up an acquaintance by asking for a light, and then that he'll find another foreigner at a loose end in Paris. Yes, I think I can play that part."

"You may think my scheme sounds a bit fantastic, but I'm sure that our next job is to find out what made those three rascals call upon Pinet at le Pecq."

They had reached their hotel. The little *chasseur* came forward. "A gentleman has been here twice asking for you, messieurs."

"A French gentleman?"

The *chasseur* nodded. "He said he would call round again in a few minutes."

"It must be M. Verneuil," whispered Richardson. "We must stick close to the hotel now until he comes."

They had not long to wait. The ex-petty officer threw his bulk against the revolving door and came forward to shake hands with them. "I thought that you had been run over by a taxi, and that the proper place to find you would be in the accident ward at one of the hospitals."

Richardson explained that they had had to attend the funeral of Everett at Père la Chaise and had only just got away.

"I went round to that hotel off the rue de Rivoli; I have copies of the *fiche* of each of those men. Here they are."

Richardson scanned them. "Ivan Novikoff; that might be Polowski's *alias*; he's a Russian now, not a Pole. Born in Riga in 1883; jeweller. 'Septimus Zizon,' born in Roumania in 1890, jeweller. 'Richard Small.' This fellow doesn't seem to have filled in his form."

"No, monsieur. The manageress said that he had declined to do so. I told her that when the men came in she should say that in the course of his weekly visit round the hotels the police *commissaire* had noticed this and had told her to insist on the form being completed, and if he declined he would be called down to the police station to be interrogated. I could even have him called down now, but I desired to consult you gentlemen first."

"You did well, monsieur; it may suit us better not to alarm the men by taking any police action against them at this stage." Richardson went on to hint at the possibility that they might approach Cooper in a café and try to victimize him.

Verneuil treated this as an immense joke. "At what café do you propose to set this snare? I should like to be there to see it work."

"At the Café Veil, not this evening, but tomorrow at the hour of the *apéritif.*"

"I shall be there, messieurs—not, of course, in the company of M. Cooper, but as a humble member of the audience at this comedy. But the attractive lady you mention—the lady who is to wink at M. Cooper? Who is she to be?"

"We were trusting to luck for the lady, monsieur; ladies of that kind are not hard to find at the hour of the *apéritif.*"

"No; there is a sufficiency, but she may prove to be an embarrassment in your comedy. Why should you not allow me to provide the lady—a member of our official staff, and quite attractive enough to prove the downfall of M. Cooper."

In this manner everything was arranged. Cooper and the lady were to arrive at their posts at a quarter to seven on the following evening. There remained only the question of Cooper's make-up, and this was put off until the interview with Mr. Gregory on the following morning.

"How shall I know the lady?" asked Cooper.

"I shall bring her to the café myself at a quarter to seven, place her at a table not far from yours and leave her there, after pointing you out to her."

Chapter Ten

THE TWO English detectives sat up late discussing their plan.

"The first thing to do to-morrow morning, Cooper," said Richardson, "is for you to change your hotel. I've asked on the quiet what kind of hotel a young spendthrift rip like you would choose for a hectic week in Paris, and I'm told that the Grand in the Avenue de l'Opéra is the very place. It won't take us long to pay your bill here, and for me to engage your room at the Grand Hotel as if you were a friend arriving from England. Then we'll go round to the Embassy and ask Mr. Gregory's advice about your make-up. He may even let you change either in the Embassy or at his private flat. We've got to make you look reckless."

"But when I've struck up an acquaintance with Polowski, where am I to receive him when he calls?"

"In your private room at the Grand, of course. We'll have to run to a private sitting-room where you can stretch out at full length on a lounge with an empty champagne bottle beside you, looking as if you were just getting over a big debauch. Now you'd better get to bed and wake up fresh; you've got an exciting day before you."

At ten o'clock next morning the two arrived at the Embassy and asked Chubb for Mr. Gregory.

"You've hit off the time exactly," said that functionary; "he's just come in—a good fifteen minutes before his regular time. I'll take you right in; there'll be no one there except Mr. Dundas, and he'll take his telegrams into another room to decode. Lord bless you! He can't do a thing if people are talking."

Ned Gregory rose in welcoming fashion, "I couldn't get to sleep last night, inspector, for wondering what this great plan of yours was."

"No, sir? The plan is quite simple. In rough outline it is this: Sergeant Cooper is to take up his position in front of the Café Veil at the time of the *apéritif,* in the hope that the three rascals I told you about will be there. He is to make friends with them if he can and induce them to become confidential. We want to make him up in the character of a dissolute young Englishman who has come over to Paris to amuse himself regardless of expense. He is to be the son of a West-End jeweller who died some weeks ago, leaving everything to his widow with a reversion to his son.

The widow dotes upon her only child. That would make him fair game for any swindle these rogues are plotting."

"In your place I should shift the parents over to Canada and make them French Canadians in a big way of business."

"How would he dress the part?"

"Oh, that's easy; we have dozens of them in here, or rather we used to before Canada went off gold—a big black slouched hat, such as some French artists affect, a blue tie fastened in a bow, and clothes of outlandish cut. Look here, why shouldn't you turn over his make-up to me? He can dress in my rooms, and I'll get together everything that's necessary. The clothes would be reach-me-downs; they need not be a perfect fit. What are your height and chest measurements, Mr. Cooper?" Cooper supplied them. "Good! Is it to be for this evening or to-morrow?"

"This evening, we thought," said Richardson. "We've already taken Mr. Cooper's rooms at the Grand Hotel."

"Couldn't be better. Here's the address of my flat. You'd better be round there not later than half-past four; that'll give you time to change and stick your luggage on a taxi and drive to the Grand Hotel. You hail from Quebec. Are you going to be at the Café Veil too, inspector?"

"No, sir. This is essentially a one-man job."

"If you see me in the offing at the Café Veil this evening, it won't put you off your stroke?" asked Gregory with a grin. "To me it would be far more amusing than any play."

"Not at all, sir; you might eventually come into the case as a witness for the prosecution by identifying the men."

"I should plead diplomatic immunity. Well, then, that's settled. Are you going to take a holiday, inspector?"

"No, sir, I have a very dull job on hand. If Verneuil can arrange it, I'm going to take every scrap of paper that was found in Mr. Everett's flat and go through it again." He turned to Cooper. "You remember that case of mine—the case of Naomi

Clynes? Well, it was a sheet of paper that would have hanged John Maze if he hadn't taken cyanide to escape the hangman."

"Don't forget, half-past four at my flat," said Gregory as they rose to go.

"No, sir; I shall see that he's punctual. I should like very much, if I may, to come upstairs and see him in all his war-paint," said Richardson.

"Why, of course! He has the address; all you have to do is to ring the bell."

Richardson and Cooper's next visit was to M. Verneuil at the police station. He wilted a little at Richardson's request to be allowed to carry papers out of the office, but when it was explained to him that his British colleague was going to work at them until past midnight if necessary, and would undertake to return them intact, his objections were removed.

"All I ask, monsieur, is that you should not mention this to M. Bigot when you happen to see him. He's a little over prone to fault-finding, and if you don't mind, I must ask you to come here at four o'clock to receive them."

Thus it was that by the time Richardson had returned to the hotel with the papers, Cooper had already left for Ned Gregory's flat, which had been turned into a green room for the occasion.

Having stowed the papers in his locked valise and locked the door of his cupboard, Richardson went down to the office to settle his colleague's bill.

"Your friend is returning to England, monsieur?" inquired the manageress, who in these straitened times looked upon the departure of a client as a nail in the coffin of her hostelry.

"He has to go on a journey," replied Richardson evasively; "he may be back in a few days. Will you have his valise put on a taxi? I am going to see him off."

The taxi was directed to drive with Cooper's luggage to Ned Gregory's flat. The *concierge* directed Richardson to the *appartement* on the left.

"He has a gentleman with him," she said.

"Yes, and this is that gentleman's luggage. Please take care of it till he comes down."

Arrived on the second floor, Richardson shut the gates and sent the lift down. He rang the bell; a *bonne* opened the door.

"Monsieur is engaged with a gentleman," she said.

"Yes, but he is expecting me. Please take him this card."

From an inner room a head was protruded with caution; it was a well-groomed red head. Reassured by a glance at his visitor, Gregory came forward with a welcoming enthusiasm. "You're just in time, inspector. I want to introduce you to my friend from Quebec, the son of a wealthy French Canadian."

He threw open the door of the inner room like a showman, and Richardson started back with an involuntary exclamation. "Let me present to you M. Rivaux, inspector; I don't think you have ever met him before."

The apparition who answered to the name of Rivaux was less remarkable in Paris than he would have been in London. He was wearing a soft black hat with a vast brim, which he swept off on the introduction, disclosing the luxuriant black hair of a wig that might well have been by Clarkson. His suit might equally well have been by anyone but a London tailor.

"I must get you photographed," was Richardson's only comment, and then, feeling that commendation must not be withheld from the costumier, he turned to Ned Gregory and said that it was a marvellous transformation.

"What I was aiming at, you see," said Gregory modestly, "was to produce something that would at once attract attention in a crowded café."

"You have certainly succeeded, sir."

"I've been impressing on Mr. Cooper that he must walk into the place as if it belonged to him, and order the waiters about with the air of a man who has money to burn."

"You needn't be afraid, inspector," said Cooper. "Thanks to Mr. Gregory, I think I know my part. He has even given me a hint of the proper accent, for it seems that French Canadians pronounce French as they did in the time of Louis the Fourteenth."

"It's early yet," said Gregory. "I'm going to order some tea, and while we're drinking it we'll continue the lesson in French as she is spoke in Quebec until it's time for you to start for the Café Veil."

"And I'll go back to my hotel and tackle those papers. I can get them done this evening."

"Shall I come and report to you at your hotel, inspector?" asked Cooper.

"No, that wouldn't do at all. They might be following you, and the manageress might penetrate your disguise. No, I'll come and see you at the Grand Hotel at ten o'clock."

On Richardson's departure Ned Gregory turned schoolmaster again, and he found Cooper an apt pupil. As the hands of the clock approached half-past six he rose. "I think you had better be moving, Mr. Cooper. You haven't forgotten your Canadian name, I hope?"

"No, sir; I'm Jacques Rivaux, and my address is 16 rue Royale, Quebec. I came over in the steamer *Voyageur*. I'm disappointed in Paris; I've been to show after show and they're all alike—nothing but girls with flying legs. If you've seen one you've seen all. It's dull here, I think."

"Very good indeed; that's the line to take. As you will have a lady with you during the latter part of Act I, you will find it easier to splash your money about. If you happen to notice me in the front row of the stalls, don't be tempted to wink at me!"

On his taxi-drive to the Café Veil, Cooper was a prey to the fear that all these well-laid plans might be brought to nought through the absence of the three miscreants, but as his driver swung round the corner to set him down, his heart beat fast, for he had caught sight of the trio seated at their former table. Paying his fare, he proceeded to swagger into the alley-way, and was conscious of the interest he was exciting, not only among his little party, but among all the occupied tables within ten yards of him. The waiter invited him to a table in the same section as that of the three. He gave his order. A few moments later, M. Verneuil made his appearance, accompanied by a striking-looking dame, not, it must be confessed, in her first youth, but admirably gowned and groomed. The ex-petty officer hesitated and looked puzzled. Cooper realized that his disguise was too perfect for recognition, but he dared not make a sign because his little group had begun to take an unhealthy interest in him. Fortunately the lady herself went straight to the only vacant table and sat down, and this gave Cooper an excuse for looking in her direction with the faintest suggestion of a wink, his face being turned away from Polowski and his friends. Verneuil took ceremonious leave of his fair companion and departed.

Cooper seemed to be quite an adept at ogling; he was glad to find that the lady was as well posted in her part as he—she kept glancing at him and looking away whenever he caught her eye. When his eye was elsewhere, she brought the full battery of her charms to bear on him. Presently, when there was no waiter within call, she took out a cigarette, fitted it into a holder, and felt in her bag for a light. She clicked her tongue petulantly and looked round for the waiter. Cooper sprang from his chair, and removing his wide-brimmed hat with a sweep, produced a lighter. The lady made use of it and thanked him with a gracious smile. Cooper pointed inquiringly to the vacant chair by her side; she begged him to be seated.

He found that she was quite a remarkable impersonator. While appearing to deal in all the arts of coquetry, her conversation would have greatly surprised Polowski and his friends if they could have overheard it.

"Are the people here?" she asked.

"Yes," replied Cooper, playing up to her with an enamoured look. "I'll tell you where they're sitting; don't look round, because they're staring at us. They are at the third table at the back, beyond the alley-way."

"The third table: I'll see them when we get up to go."

"Have you worked long in connection with the detective service in Paris?"

"For several months, off and on, sometimes for M. Bigot, more often for M. Verneuil. He amuses me, that gentleman—a typical sailor. And you, monsieur? They tell me that you belong to your famous Scotland Yard of which we read in the *roman feuilleton*."

"It is a great pleasure to an English detective to make the acquaintance of so astute a lady as yourself," said Cooper gallantly. "Let me offer you an *apéritif*."

"Thank you, monsieur. I have to keep to my regime; I've had the only beverage that I permit myself to take. Shall we put your friends over there to the test? If you will look across the street you will see a small jeweller's shop. I suggest that we pay the waiter and cross over to it. If your friends follow us, then our mission will have been successful; if not, we must try some other ruse. You wish to impress them with the idea that you are a reckless young Canadian with his pockets full of money, is it not so? Well, a rich young Canadian would naturally desire to give the lady of his choice some mark of his esteem. You, however, like myself, have no money to throw away, but it costs us nothing to enter a jeweller's and inquire the price of his wares. I have here a little box wrapped in paper which you will appear to have given me. Shall we go? I want to look at these gentlemen as I go out—the third table from the alley-way, you say?"

With a lingering gaze into Cooper's eyes she rose, and he stood aside to let her pass him, observing only that she cast a glance in the direction of Polowski before gaining the pavement. Cooper did not dare to look behind him, but some subtle instinct told him Polowski was also on the move. The lady crossed the street with the superb indifference to the risk of oncoming traffic that distinguishes most Parisians and halted before the jeweller's window. She pointed with a gloved finger at jewels that seemed to take her fancy; she leaned towards Cooper as if he was the romantic hero of her girlhood, and then Cooper appeared to be persuading her to enter the shop with him and to overcome her scruples, for from the corner of his eye he had seen the Polowski group streaming over the road in their direction. It may be supposed that Paris jewellers are accustomed to foreigners who admire and ask prices, but do not buy, for this one was tireless in displaying glittering gewgaws. Cooper admired, but his admiration did not prevent him from glancing towards the plate-glass window where his three villains were apparently intent on the jewels displayed. At a hint from his companion, Cooper said that he hoped to visit the shop again by daylight. As they turned to go the lady produced a little parcel from her bag, made up in the form used by jewellers for their goods.

"You gave me this, *mon chéri*; how can I show my gratitude to you—a man so generous?" She was in the doorway when she turned to address Cooper in this flattering fashion, and as he followed her out one of the three men seemed purposely to cannon against him.

"*Milles pardons, monsieur!*" cried the man, removing his hat in confusion.

"It is nothing, monsieur," said Cooper, sweeping off his imposing headgear with a flourish.

The man tried to continue the conversation, but with a bow Cooper hurried on to overtake his companion, who was walking in the direction of the Madeleine. He had now the exquisite satisfaction of knowing that the rôles were reversed; that he, a detective of the Central Division at Scotland Yard, was being shadowed by three of the most shameless rascals in Europe.

"They are following us," murmured the lady, without looking round. She had surveyed the pavement behind them in a mirror in one of the shop windows.

"Yes; that's a hopeful sign, but we must shake them off."

"Nothing easier," said she, stopping at the taxi rank and mounting the step of a taxi. She gave their destination in a clear voice which, if it did not carry as far as their pursuers, was heard by all the other drivers in the rank.

"The Restaurant Marly."

Their taxi sped away towards the Champs-Élysées.

"What is your destination, monsieur? The Grand Hotel? Then I'm taking you out of your way. I live on the other side of the river."

"Then," said Cooper gallantly, "let me drive you home."

"Thank you, monsieur, but I prefer to take the Metro." She tapped on the window and signed to the driver to stop. "I shall be quite safe in getting down here," she said; "there is the station of the Rond Point just opposite." She looked through the back window. "They didn't take the trouble to follow our taxi. Will you want me tomorrow?"

"Probably not, madame, but if I should, I will telephone to M. Verneuil a little after six."

"*Au revoir, monsieur.*"

Cooper directed the taxi-man to drive to the Grand Hotel. He walked to the desk and said that a friend had taken a room for him that afternoon.

"Your name, monsieur?"

"Jacques Rivaux."

"Quite correct, monsieur," agreed the clerk, and signalling to a *chasseur*, he gave directions for the luggage to be taken up to Number 33. He put a registration form before Cooper and invited him to fill it up. Quick reflection told Cooper that it would be unsatisfactory if he filled up the form in a disguised hand. The question of his handwriting was never likely to arise in the future. He supposed that these forms were useful in exceptional cases, but that as a general rule they were never looked at by the police. He filled his form up with a complete disregard for the truth, trusting that his police friends would be there to exonerate him if the form were ever called in question.

He was conducted to a room on the first floor. He had never bargained for so much luxury. The bathroom, with its enormous porcelain bath in which one might easily drown oneself; the huge pedestal wash-hand basin and the ante-room which could serve as a sitting-room, were all of the most modern kind. He looked into cupboard after cupboard and found each furnished with some unexpected gadget. Even in the bathroom the towels were kept warm in a little closet fitted with an electric coil. It was the sort of palatial lodging that a dissipated Canadian millionaire's son might well affect.

Cooper was hungry. It did not worry him that his outfit was not such as is frequently seen in the dining-room of the Grand Hotel, but what would you? No Canadian millionaire's son could go without his dinner. He must play the part. He played the part right royally.

Having satisfied his appetite, it only remained to await the arrival of his chief; he passed the time in rehearsing the interview with Polowski on which he was counting for the next day. He had begun to feel confidence in his powers; perhaps the wine imbibed at dinner had given him courage. At ten o'clock the telephone bell rang and a voice informed him that a gentleman was asking for M. Rivaux from Quebec.

"Show him up, please," was Cooper's reply. A knock at the door, the turning of a key, the closing of the door behind the guest, and Richardson stood before him, surveying the room with an appraising eye.

"Doing yourself pretty well, Sergeant Cooper," he said. "I hope that it's not going to give you expensive tastes."

"No fear of that, inspector, but you see, one has to play up to the part."

"And how did your little comedy go?"

Cooper related his adventure at the Café Veil and at the jeweller's opposite.

"You are sure that you saw them following you?" asked Richardson.

"Quite sure, and so was M. Verneuil's lady."

"Did she play her part well?"

"She couldn't have done it better."

"And that Roumanian chap barged up against you, did he? Well, that's a good sign. If you're in your place at the café to-morrow, one of them will sidle up to you and start the ball rolling. You'd better not change your kit to-morrow, because if you did they mightn't recognize you again; nor would it do for the hotel people to see you decently dressed and in your right mind. You'll have a dull day, I fear. Don't forget about the marks of dissipation, an empty champagne bottle and the rest of it if you bring them back here."

"That's all right; I've made a list of the scenery. How did you get on with those papers?"

"I went through every scrap of them and found nothing that would be of the slightest use to us."

"Then what are you going to do to-morrow?"

"Well, it occurred to me as I was walking down here that Everett must have had a writing-table, or the use of one, at the Embassy. When I've returned this lot of papers to Verneuil, I shall go and see Mr. Gregory and ask him about it. Now get to bed and don't lie awake thinking."

Chapter Eleven

M. BIGOT was receiving a visitor in his little office—a dark-complexioned young man whose hair was prematurely thin. He was protesting. "It comes to this, inspector; you were good enough to give me that story of the German Nazi dagger with which the murder was committed. My editor was delighted with it. Now he complains that the story is incomplete; that we hear no more about the dagger; yet, as you told me yourself, it was with it that the murder in the rue St. Georges was committed."

"You went much too far in your article in *Le Témoin*. I never told you that the dagger had been supplied to the murdered man by the Germans."

"I know you did not, but your story that it had been sent by a friend on the opposite side of the frontier had no publicity value whatever, whereas if it can be said that it was supplied by one of the Nazi leaders to a member of the British Embassy staff... Or even that the dead man had received a visit from a Nazi chief who came armed with this dagger —think for yourself what can be made of it! "

Bigot attempted a dash of sarcasm. "I observe that *Le Témoin* is not concerned with the truth of what it prints, only with its publicity value."

"The truth has very little to do with successful modern journalism, and, after all, who can say what is true and what is false? Two men may be watching the same incident; for example, a house painter falls from a ladder and is killed. One eye-witness will swear that he missed a rung with his foot and fell by accident; another, that he threw himself from the ladder with intention: both are recounting what they saw in good faith. The historian can choose between them."

"Yes, but..."

"I know what you are going to say—that I had no right to tell our readers that Mr. Everett received that dagger from a German Nazi, but from an English friend who wrote to him from the other side of the frontier. That is no story for a journal such as ours. If my version was not strictly true, it was better than the truth. As my editor said, if it wasn't the truth it ought to have been. The moment has now come for you to redeem your promise and tell me something more about that dagger. The public expects it."

"At this stage, monsieur, I can tell you nothing more; you will have to wait until our inquiries are complete."

The reporter of *The Witness* left the police station grumbling.

It was this conversation which led to headlines in *The Witness* of the following morning:

"THE TRAGEDY IN THE RUE ST. GEORGES
"Was the assassin armed with a German Nazi dagger, or had the victim secretly become a German Nazi propagandist?"

There followed an article, signed by the reporter, deploring the secretiveness of the police, and inviting his readers to await startling revelations when the inquiry was completed.

This was the article which First Secretary Carruthers found lying upon his table, conspicuously marked in blue pencil by Chubb. He rang the bell and Chubb entered himself.

"Did you take a copy of this rag up to His Excellency?"

"I did, sir."

"Did you mark it in blue pencil as you have marked my copy?"

"No, sir; considering His Excellency's state of health, I thought it better not to."

"You did well."

Carruthers carried the paper upstairs to the ambassador's room. He found his chief violently agitated; a copy of *Le Témoin* was lying on the table before him.

"Ah! You've seen this scandalous rag? Something must be done about it immediately. The editor must be seen and warned that any repetition of this offensive stuff will make it necessary for us to apply to the Quai d'Orsay for protection. Hadn't we better send Maynard to see the editor?"

"I should keep Maynard for appealing to the Quai d'Orsay if the editor digs in his heels and talks of the liberty of the Press. The best man for the editor would be Gregory. He knows these Pressmen, and has managed them very well so far."

"But isn't he too apt to be flippant with them?"

"Only when they require a light touch. He can be stiff enough with them when it's necessary."

"Very well, send Gregory, and please let me see him when he comes back."

Ned Gregory took a taxi to the imposing office of *Le Témoin* in the rue Sebastopol and sent in his card to the editor. He was not kept waiting long; a well-groomed young man hurried into the waiting-room and introduced himself as the editor's secretary. He said, "The editor has been called away, monsieur; he will be desolated at not seeing you. Is there anything I can do?"

Gregory drew a mental picture of the editor, either cowering in the editorial chair or seizing his hat and slipping out unobtrusively by a back staircase into the street. His reply seemed to be a facer. "You are very good, monsieur, but my business can only be dealt with by a personal interview with the editor. I feel sure that if an effort is made there will be little difficulty in communicating with him by telephone." He took out his watch. "If you will allow me I will make a note of the time I am kept waiting for the interview; if it is unduly long it is possible that the British ambassador, whom I am representing, may think it right to mention the fact in his representations to the Quai d'Orsay. In the meantime, with your permission, I will pass the interval in this chair."

It was a chastened private secretary who received this ultimatum. "Certainly, monsieur. I will at once take steps to communicate with the editor if he can be found; but I may have difficulty. Paris is a large city."

Gregory amused himself with calculations. What would be the minimum time they would dare to keep him waiting, consistent with saving the face of the secretary, who had asserted that the editor was keeping an appointment in another part of Paris? He decided that from seven to ten minutes would be resolved upon, and that he would then be faced with a gentleman a little breathless with haste, profuse in apologies for the delay which had been forced upon him by circumstances over which he had had no control. If only he had known beforehand…

It was just seven minutes when a quick step in the passage announced the return of the private secretary. He was wreathed in smiles. "I have been lucky, monsieur. After one or two abortive calls on the telephone I got into touch with the editor. He took a taxi at once. He has just arrived. If you will come this way…"

Gregory was ushered into the editorial sanctum—a big room which seemed to be reserved for receiving distinguished visitors or for board meetings, for its only furniture besides the writing-table was a row of handsome, leather-covered chairs against the wall. A cadaverous little man with a complexion like dirty creased paper rose from his chair and came hurrying towards his visitor with outstretched hand. He was a little out of breath.

"I ask a thousand pardons, monsieur, for having unwittingly kept you waiting, but you know what it is. The editor of a great daily newspaper is never allowed to call his time his own." He scurried away to the row of chairs and brought one up to the table.

"Please give yourself the trouble to sit down and tell me what I can do for you."

Ned Gregory had assumed an unwonted air of gravity. Towering above the man he had come to see, he took the chair offered him and pulled from his pocket a copy of *Le Témoin* of that morning's date, and opened it out leisurely to bring the offending column, heavily marked in blue pencil, to the front. This he laid on the table before the editor.

"The ambassador has instructed me to call your attention to this article, monsieur."

"Ah, that! His Excellency, the ambassador, takes exception to it?"

"He takes the strongest exception to it, especially to the headlines."

"Ah, the headlines... yes... I recognize at once that the headlines, which seem to have slipped through after the article was written, were ill-advised. I wish I had seen them before the paper went to press."

"It is not only the headlines, though they are bad enough, that the ambassador takes exception to; it is the article itself."

"*Tiens!* But it was written by Jacques Penaud, one of our best men."

"But it is not true."

"You surprise me, monsieur. I was assured that it had all been verified by the police who were in charge of the case; that they said that the murder had been done with a German Nazi dagger. Was that not true?"

"It was, but the dagger had long been the property of Mr. Everett, who used it as a paperknife, and he received it as a gift from an English friend who was on the other side of the German frontier. He showed it to me at the time he was given it."

"Ah! That throws an entirely different light upon the affair. I can assure you, monsieur, that if the police had told my reporter that, the ambassador would have had no cause to complain. I hope you will assure His Excellency that there will be no further reference to the matter complained of in the columns of my paper…"

Gregory had fulfilled his mission, but he could not resist the temptation to press this compliant gentleman a little further. "I fear, monsieur, that the ambassador will not be content with that assurance. If that is all you can offer it may be difficult to restrain him from applying to the Quai d'Orsay for protection, and I fancy that in these dark days representations from France's strong ally may have repercussions." If he had doubted whether the important newspapers received subsidies from the French Government, the reaction of the editor convinced him of it.

"What more can I do, monsieur?"

"You can insert a correction to the effect that you have been misinformed; that the dagger used by the murderer of Mr. Everett had been a long time in the possession of the murdered man, who used it as a paper-knife, and that you regret having been misled. *Tenez, monsieur.* I have brought with me a rough draft of the correction which I suggest you should insert."

He pulled from his pocket-book a slip of paper with a few lines of typescript. The editor read it with knitted brows.

"Very well, monsieur; a correction on these lines will appear in to-morrow's issue."

"Pardon me, monsieur; it must not be only on these lines, but in these words, and it must appear in the same position and the same type as the original paragraph."

A noble resignation took charge of the editor's features as he consented.

As Ned Gregory descended the steps into the street he narrowly escaped colliding with Inspector Bigot, who was entering the building in plain clothes. Bigot stopped him, saying, "I am not surprised to see you here, monsieur. Like me, you have been here to protest against that disgraceful article in this morning's paper."

Ned Gregory's manner was cool. "You think the article disgraceful? Yet the editor tells me that his reporter got his information from you or from one of your subordinates."

The inspector recoiled as if from a blow in the face. "Impossible! Did he dare say that? Why, I myself have come to protest in the strongest terms. I do not remember ever having seen the man who signs the article."

"Ah!"

"No, monsieur. I hope that you will assure His Excellency the ambassador that we are maintaining the strictest reserve; that I consider the article disgraceful, and that I have come specially to see the editor to protest against it."

"I am glad to hear it, monsieur," replied Gregory, signalling to a taxi. "*Au revoir*, monsieur the inspector."

Unlike Ned Gregory, Bigot was not made to wait for his interview. He was admitted to the sanctum at once. The editor motioned him to the chair vacated by Gregory without rising.

"Well," said he, "what is it now?"

"I have come to protest against that article in the paper this morning."

"What is wrong with it?"

"Wrong with it? Why, it's not true."

"How do *you* know that it's not true? You were paid for the information you gave me, weren't you? Well, stranger things than what appeared in this morning's paper have proved in the end to be true."

"Yes, but...listen, monsieur, if you will give a *démenti* to that article, I can promise you exclusive information about the real murderer of the English diplomat, and I can promise you a startling sensation. When my new case is complete, and it involves a deputy, nay more, a Minister, what would you not give for the exclusive information? And I should make no stipulation against allowing my name to appear as the officer who conducted the inquiry."

"Very well, inspector, if you are successful you can come to me."

Ned Gregory returned to the Embassy and entered the first secretary's room.

"What, back already? Did you have any luck?" was Carruthers' greeting.

Gregory related his experiences at the office of *Le Témoin*.

"You seem to have greatly exceeded your instructions, young man," said his senior in mock reproof. "You were never told to frighten the editor into inserting a *démenti* in to-morrow's issue and drafting it yourself."

"He was badly frightened when I told him that the ambassador contemplated going to the Quai d'Orsay. He saw his Government subsidy melting away."

"You had better go straight upstairs to H.E. and tell him all about it. He said particularly that he wanted to see you as soon as you came back."

Gregory ran upstairs and knocked at the ambassador's door. He found his chief in the mood for receiving fresh blows. "Sit down and tell me the worst," he said.

Gregory's version of his interview lost nothing in the telling. The poor ambassador, who had been sunk in his chair with a fresh access of internal trouble, gradually became sound again, as he did to the stimulus of one of his doctor's remedies. He was even almost jubilant when Gregory related the pressure he had brought to bear upon the editor to insert a *démenti* in the next issue of his paper.

"You drafted the terms of the *démenti* yourself?"

"Yes, sir, I thought it would meet with your approval if I did."

"You have done very well indeed, Mr. Gregory. If only we could get those detectives from Scotland Yard to get a move on, I should feel that we were accomplishing something. Do you see anything of them?"

"Yes, sir; I think they are doing everything possible under the circumstances. They are following a trail now which promises well. It would not be fair to them to tell anybody what it is, but their policy seems to me likely to end in bringing home the crime to the right person."

Chapter Twelve

WHEN COOPER arrived at the café next evening the three were in their places. They appeared to take no notice of him. He had scarcely given his order when he saw with some concern that Ned Gregory was occupying a table against the window, two or three yards away. For a moment it seemed to spoil his stroke, but that feeling soon gave way to the encouragement which an appreciative audience exercises on the actor. In any case he had no time for reflection, for at that moment the Polowski party was breaking up. The Roumanian and the pugilist were taking a ceremonious leave of Polowski—hats off, bows, handshakes and smiles, as if the trio were destined to be parted for ever. Polowski was now alone; so was Cooper. What more natural than that these two lonely men should be drawn together. It was Polowski's need of a light for his cigarette that did the drawing. Actually Cooper was looking the other way when a soft, insinuating voice accosted him, asking for a match. Cooper, or rather Rivaux, was not one of those travellers who keep their fellow-men at arm's length. On the contrary, he himself struck the light and handed it to Polowski with a flourish.

"Have you been long in Paris?" asked the Pole.

Rivaux motioned him to take the chair beside him. "Several weeks now—quite long enough to be bored stiff. I remember when I came over for my education my dream was to come back to Paris with money in my pocket, and now that my dream is realized I wish I'd stayed at home. Say, are you a Frenchman?"

"No, I'm from Warsaw."

"I'm glad to hear it. I shouldn't like to belittle Paris to a Frenchman, but it's a dull sort of place."

"Have you been to the shows?"

"Yes, half a dozen of them, and they're all alike; nothing but half-naked girls kicking up their legs and grinning at you. And the cinemas are nearly as bad. Why, you can't open a paper in this country to read about a nice, brutal crime without having a girl dragged into it."

"Well, young women play an important part in Paris. I believe you were here yesterday with a very attractive-looking lady. Don't tell me that she was your cousin or your niece."

Cooper laughed bitterly. "Not at all. I'd never seen her before, but you know what it is. The only thing these Paris girls want is to have money spent on them. She was an expensive handful, I can tell you. Her particular weakness was jewellery."

"Well, one need not indulge their weaknesses."

"Ah, then it's clear that you've never met that particular dame. You wouldn't escape so easily from her clutches."

"You'll forgive me for saying so, but I can't understand spending good money on these women, when, invested in a proper way, it may bring you in a fortune, and give you an interest in life into the bargain."

"But I don't care about making fortunes. I have all the money I want."

"No one has all the money he wants. The more he has the more he wants. Look at the power money gives a man, especially in this country."

Cooper laughed harshly. "It's a funny time to be talking about making money in France when everyone's going bankrupt."

"Ah! But the money I'm talking about isn't made here. It comes from Russia."

"Bolshevist money, do you mean?"

Polowski laughed softly. "No; if the Bolsheviki knew what was going on under their noses, some of us would, as they say in England, 'get it in the neck.' But that's half the attraction in the business. You are not a Frenchman, either?"

"Ah! You have not noticed my accent. By descent I am French all right. I'm a French Canadian."

"Oh! That explains it. When I first noticed you I said to my friends, 'Look round this café. Can you point out any intelligent-looking man except one?' And they replied, 'Yes, that man in the big hat. He's got brains.' They were indicating you, monsieur. I don't care to trust secrets to any but men with brains."

Polowski signalled to a waiter who was passing. "Will you join me in a drink, monsieur? What shall it be?"

"You are very kind. I will take a *byrrh-cassis*."

The drinks were ordered. Polowski pulled his chair a few inches nearer to his new acquaintance and became confidential. "My friends and I have been handling a very remunerative business. You have heard of the gold-mines in the Urals? Well, a Russian friend of ours was approached by the superintendent of the mines, who found it quite easy to transfer parcels of gold to my friend to be sold abroad. You know how the price of bar gold has been soaring up?"

Cooper yawned as though he were not interested.

Polowski continued, "The man we used to deal with in Paris has died at a most inconvenient moment, in fact, just when we have a consignment to dispose of cheap. Somehow, we must effect a sale, and we do not know who to employ."

"Why not take it to a bank and sell it openly?"

"Ah! You do not know the risk we should be running. They'd question us for hours about where the stuff came from. They have ways of knowing gold from the Urals from other gold. It would cost our Russian friend his life. But I can see that you are a man who can be trusted with a secret. You must know numbers of substantial people in Canada who would be glad to purchase the stuff for fifty per cent, of its value. If you consented to come in with us, I can guarantee that in a very few months you would realize a fortune. You see, we have to get back to Poland to meet our friend on the frontier, and we want a man we can trust to dispose of the metal we brought over with us."

"That's all very well, but suppose I do find a purchaser, how am I going to get the gold over to Canada?"

"That's part of the fun—a spice of adventure—and you with your intelligence and your Canadian connections could do it, while we can't."

"I would have to know a lot more about the business before I came in."

"Of course you would. Only a fool would come into a business like this before he's tested it with his own eyes and knew the people he was dealing with. I'll tell you what I could do. You appoint a time and place, and I'll bring a sample of the goods together with the means for testing it. You can make the test yourself."

"Yes, but remember that I've got to run a risk. If they found the gold on me at the Canadian Customs, they'd give me a hell of a time for not declaring it."

"That, as I said before, is your affair. Only one thing I must insist upon—that if you are stopped and questioned you'll refuse to say anything about the mines in the Urals: that would mean consigning two or three people to death by torture."

Cooper seemed to weigh the pros and cons. "If I were to come into the business it would be for the adventure, not for the profits one would make. It would amuse me to do a bit of smuggling."

Polowski sank his voice. "We'll start in quite a small way. I suppose you could lay your hands on £5,000 easily enough, just as a trial trip which will bring you in £10,000. Then, if you're successful, we could double the amount of the next consignment."

"Am I the only man in France who knows about this business? Should I be your only agent?"

"Yes, but I ought to tell you that we have approached one man, a Frenchman, before I met you, only we haven't told him where the stuff comes from. You know what these Frenchmen are—a great deal of talk and very little do when it comes to the point. Now it's different dealing with a man like you."

"I don't altogether like playing second fiddle to a French guy."

"Oh, but we turned him down at once. You needn't consider him in any way at all. Now, to show you the confidence I have in you I'll give you this." He pulled out of his vest pocket a tiny object wrapped in tissue-paper, and opened it out, disclosing a little nugget of water-worn gold. "You can take this round to any jeweller you like to choose and get him to test it. You needn't even bother to return it to me if you'd like to keep it. When would it suit you to let me come round to your hotel with a bigger sample? To-morrow morning?"

"No, not in the morning. Why not the afternoon at half-past two?"

"That's all right for me, but who shall I ask for? We've been talking intimately, but I do not know your name and you don't know mine." He pulled a card from his pocket on which was inscribed "Ivan Novikoff."

Cooper felt a glow of gratitude to his inspector for his foresight in providing him with a visiting-card, "Jacques Rivaux, Quebec." They exchanged cards.

Polowski stopped the waiter and paid his bill. Jumping to his feet he swept off his hat and took a ceremonious farewell. "At half-past two tomorrow. *Au revoir*, monsieur."

When he had departed in the direction of the Madeleine, Cooper looked round. The chairs lately occupied by his friends were empty. He walked down the Boulevard in the opposite direction and made straight for the Grand Hotel. He called for his key at the desk, and was crossing the hall towards the lift when he caught sight of a red head. Its owner was seated beside Richardson. They made no sign of recognition; they left him to ascend in the lift, and a moment later the telephone bell in Number 33 began to tinkle.

"Two gentlemen to see you, monsieur. Shall I show them up?"

"Yes, please."

Richardson and Ned Gregory were shown in. Gregory surveyed his handiwork and turned to Richardson.

"Look at him, inspector. Isn't he the rich young Canadian blackguard to the life?"

"Yes, sir; your make-up was splendid, and when I saw our friend here exchanging visiting-cards with Polowski, I felt sure that our little plan had been successful. Now, Cooper, tell us how you got on."

"Well, here's the first earnest of our deal." He pulled from his pocket the little gold nugget. "He gave me this as a sample of what he's going to bring me at half-past two to-morrow afternoon. He told me that I could take it round to any jeweller to be tested."

Ned Gregory weighed it in his hand and passed it to Richardson. "It looks and feels genuine enough, but where did he say it came from?"

"From a gold-mine in the Ural Mountains."

"This never came out of a mine; it's not reef gold at all; it's water-worn, so that's lie number one," said Richardson.

"He wants me to buy £5,000 worth as a start." Cooper related the conversation he had had with Polowski in detail.

"It's a variation from the story he used to tell in London, but practically it comes to the same thing," said Richardson. "You got nothing out of him about his object in visiting Pinet?"

"No, I didn't like to press him too far. He said that he had approached a Frenchman to become his agent before he came to me, and I suppose that he was referring to Pinet. Are you going to the French police about the gang?"

"I don't want to butt in, inspector," said Gregory, "you know your own affairs best, but I do hope that you'll see the business through."

"Oh, I'm not going to hurry things. Of course, the gold will prove to be false, but the French police wouldn't take any action beyond perhaps interrogating the men and telling them to clear out of the country."

"You're right about that," said Gregory. "This is the land of asylum and liberty. With them it would be a case of *caveat emptor*—which is Latin for 'fools must look after themselves' and not come crying to the police every time they're robbed."

"I did think of getting our friend Verneuil to call upon Pinet and shake the truth out of him about the object of Polowski's visit," said Richardson. "It would be a useful check upon any story that they may tell to Cooper."

"What puzzles me," said Gregory, "is why they should go to a starveling journalist hoping to get £5,000 out of him. Our rich young friend here is quite another proposition."

"I think, sir, that we'll find they went to him *because* he is a journalist and might be able to put them on to a likely buyer by a paragraph in his paper."

"I see you coming," said Gregory. "If they wanted to get in with the French Press they might well have approached poor Everett, feeling sure that he would know the steps to take."

"Yes, sir, and in that case Mr. Everett might have thrown them out or have threatened to expose them by a hint to the French police."

"Before half-past two to-morrow I must have instructions how far I am to carry the deal," said Cooper.

"That's quite simple; you must play for time. They won't expect you to have £5,000 about you. You'll say that you have to get it over from Canada by cable through your bank, and that as soon as you have the money you'll let them know, and they will deliver the goods to you here. If we can establish the fact that they knew Everett, we could then get the French police to hold them on the swindling charge, while we work up the evidence against them for the murder."

"Well," said Gregory, "I have to thank you gentlemen for a most interesting afternoon—it's been better than any play—but I must confess frankly that I've a sinking feeling here"—he touched a spot a little below his heart—" and there's only one remedy for it—dinner. So I'll wish you good evening, and trust to you not keeping me in suspense too long to-morrow. Good night."

Left to themselves, the two detectives began to discuss their case.

"Did you find that Mr. Everett had a writing-table of his own at the Embassy?" inquired Cooper.

"Yes, a table with a locked drawer in it. Mr. Gregory rang up a locksmith and got it opened in my presence. It was packed full of papers—news-cuttings, manuscripts, carbon copies, and odds and ends."

"Nothing interesting?"

"Well, yes; there was a little engagement-book. I have it here." It was a leather-bound small book in diary form. "There are gaps in it, as you see; these journalists are always unmethodical. But there are notes of luncheons and dinners and appointments. I've been through the names, but none of them have turned up in the case. Then there are a few little personal notes scribbled at the bottom of the pages, such as the address of his bootmaker, and after the middle of July the book does not seem to have been used. There is only one entry after that. Here it is, September 9th. It's a row of figures, 070564/I8."

"Well, that's funny! Could it be the number of a cheque?"

"It might be, but why should it be entered when the book had been discontinued two months before?"

"Can you follow it up?"

"Yes. To-morrow I shall go round to Mr. Everett's bank and find out whether he drew or paid in a cheque which bore this number. As soon as I have done that I shall go round to the police station, dig out Verneuil, and get him to go down to le Pecq and tackle Pinet about the real reason why these rascals called on him two days ago."

"Well, then, we've both got our work cut out for us. After I've got rid of my visitors to-morrow afternoon I shall wait in for you."

It being a wise precaution not to be seen together in any public place such as a restaurant, the two dined separately that evening.

Chapter Thirteen

AT HALF-PAST two on the following afternoon Cooper received two visitors—Polowski and his Roumanian accomplice. Cooper scanned this gentleman with interest, for he had never had speech with him. He was a rather portly little man of Hebraic features.

"This is my friend, M. Zizon," explained Polowski. "He is one of the best-known jewellers in Bucharest; you can have the fullest confidence in him."

True to the character of Rivaux the spendthrift Canadian, Cooper had been stretched in a lounge chair with an empty champagne bottle and a glass within reach of his hand. He appeared to be only half awake. When he offered to ring for refreshments the offer was waved aside. "Thank you, no, monsieur. We have come on strict business; we must keep our brains clear."

From the recesses of his overcoat Polowski produced a brick-shaped piece of yellow metal, saying, "This is a sample of the consignment. I wish to have it tested in your presence. This gentleman has brought with him a flask of *aqua fortis* with which he will make the test under your own eyes. You have the little nugget of gold I gave you yesterday?"

"I have it here," said Cooper.

"You've had time to think over my proposition. I can see that you have, for you are a clever man and I like dealing with clever men. Now, M. Zizon, you might begin by testing this little nugget. Do the test on the table here. We do not wish to derange this gentleman."

The Roumanian Jew fumbled in his pocket and produced a tiny phial labelled *aqua fortis* and poured from it two or three drops of the acid on to the gold nugget. There was no result.

"You see; pure gold is proof against the acid, whereas any baser metal would begin at once to bubble." He looked round the room, seeking some object in its decorations to illustrate what he said. He unhooked the gilt bracelet that held back the curtain.

"Stop!" said Cooper. "You mustn't damage the furniture."

"The mark will scarcely be seen, will it, M. Zizon?"

"No," said the Roumanian. "See, I shall wipe it off with this rag and it will leave no trace at all."

"Now, M. Zizon, show us how base metal behaves; otherwise this gentleman will be saying that your acid is only water."

Zizon took the bracelet and let fall a drop of the acid upon it; the metal instantly began to bubble.

"Yes," said Cooper; "I see your stuff is stronger than water. What about this gold brick?"

"M. Zizon will show you what happens to it when we scrape off a little of it on to this piece of glass. If the scrapings were of base metal, they would dissolve entirely before your eyes."

Zizon produced a little boring tool and set it revolving on a spot in the centre of the brick, dusting the filings on to the glass and dropping acid on to them. They remained undamaged.

"We can try any part of the brick—here, for instance," said Polowski.

The experiment was repeated.

Cooper appeared to be impressed. "Yes, the test is all right; I'm satisfied."

"What day would it suit you for us to bring the rest of the consignment and weigh it in your presence?" asked Polowski.

"Well, I don't carry £5,000 about with me. I shall have to cable to Canada and ask them to credit my bank in Paris with five or six thousand pounds, and that will take time."

"Of course; I quite understand that, but if you cable this afternoon it need only take a day or two. You know, ten thousand pounds' worth of gold, which you will receive for your five thousand, is nearly as much as one man can carry into the hotel, and then when it has to be tested and weighed—and I hold to testing it and weighing it in your presence—it will take time. But I want you to be thoroughly satisfied with us, because I hope that this will be only the beginning."

"Well, will you give me three days to bring the money over? This is Wednesday. You might ring me up on Monday and we'll make an appointment. I'm a little doubtful how to get the stuff through the Customs."

"Nothing easier. You've been over in Europe buying books, you'll tell them. You pack your gold under a few layers of books, and books weigh nearly as heavy as gold. They will open your case to look, but they're not going to take the trouble of unpacking dozens of heavy books and doing them up again. That's the way in which we bring the stuff over into France—under layers of German books."

The man who called himself Zizon was packing up his testing apparatus during this conversation; Polowski rose from his chair in order to stow his gold brick more easily in some hidden pocket in his voluminous overcoat. While thus engaged, he let his tongue run on.

"Yes; I prefer to deal with clever and intelligent men. When my friend Zizon first saw you sitting in that café on the Boulevard and pointed you out to me he said, 'That is an intelligent man.' At first sight I was not sure. I thought you might be one of those pleasure-loving foreigners who come to Paris for the sake of its good *cuisine* and its agreeable women, but when I examined your features I saw that he was right. You are a clever man, monsieur—not one of those who take things easily for granted. That is the kind of man I like to do business with—a serious man. Then it shall be Monday when I call upon you again. I shall ring you up at two o'clock to ask whether the money has arrived. The gold is heavy; I do not wish to have my journey for nothing. Now we will take our leave."

Left to himself, Cooper glanced at the electric clock on the wall. He could scarcely expect Richardson before five, for he would not risk meeting the swindlers on his way up to the room. How long was he to waste time in this expensive hotel where the rich food and the confinement were beginning to pall upon him? And how was all this expense going to throw light upon the murder of Everett? Who was going to pay for it…?

He was in the deepest depression by the time the tinkle of the telephone bell in his bedroom heralded the announcement of, "A gentleman to see you, monsieur."

The gentleman in question proved to be Inspector Richardson, who said that he had taken the precaution to inquire whether M. Rivaux was alone.

"Well," he asked, "how did it go?"

Cooper gave him a detailed account of his recent interview, not omitting the incident of the testing of the gold brick.

"That old wheeze? I expected something a little more original from a man of Polowski's experience."

"It's an old trick, then?"

"One of the oldest. I'm afraid that they neglected your education in the detective class, Cooper. If they had taken you to the museum at the Yard they would have shown you a specimen of one of these bricks—a square piece of brass with holes in it filled half an inch deep with pure gold. I suppose they didn't let you look at it too closely or you might have noticed a slight difference in the colour."

"Now I come to think of it, they didn't even let me take it in my hand, and I was so busy watching the testing experiment that I didn't think of asking for a closer view."

"Perhaps it was as well. It might have put them on their guard. The wheeze is always the same. They know where the holes are and they use a boring tool, such as a bradawl, to bore out a few shavings of gold on which they pour a few drops of the acid. You didn't ask them to let you keep the brick?"

"I didn't dare to put them off."

"I think you were right…"

"How long am I to stop here? It must be costing a little fortune. Won't there be a row when you send in the bill?"

"If it all comes to nothing there may be, but I don't think that it *will* come to nothing. Having gone so far we must see the thing through. If you were to leave the hotel now, and they came round to inquire for you and found you gone, the fat would be in the fire."

"Must I still go to that beastly café? That blighter, Polowski, will pester my life out if I do."

"No, you needn't do that; you've got to wait now until Saturday. I've been round to Everett's bank. They told me that he had neither paid in nor drawn a cheque bearing that number I showed you, but we have another string to our bow. Verneuil is off to le Pecq this evening to take Pinet by the throat and get his account of the visit of Polowski and his gang. He invited us to go with him, but I thought it might queer his pitch if we were to sit watching his methods. Verneuil is not like his chief, who likes to show off before foreigners; he has a rough and ready way with suspects and deals with them in the approved French way, which would make the pundits of our High Court gnash their teeth."

"I wouldn't mind the delay so much if there was something for me to do, but what *can* I do as long as I have to wear this beastly disguise?"

"The hat, you mean? Why, it's quite becoming to you. You must have had many worse things to do in your time than to stop in a first-class hotel in Paris with the run of your teeth. Why, most men in the department would be green with envy."

"I suppose they would until they tried it. Are you going to see Verneuil to-night after he's been to le Pecq, or to-morrow morning?"

"He's a good fellow, Verneuil; he's coming round to my hotel as soon as he gets back. I'll tell you what I'll do. I'll ring up when I've seen him and give you his report in English. Even if people listen in, they won't understand if I talk fast. And now, if you are spoiling for a job, when you've had your dinner you can turn to and write a report about what happened this afternoon."

"What's Bigot doing all this time?"

"God knows! When I ask Verneuil he screws up his eyes in that comic way he has, and his stomach begins to heave with suppressed laughter. He doesn't seem to have a lofty opinion of his chief."

"I'm not surprised," said Cooper. "Bigot strikes me as a self-important ass."

"The trouble with Bigot is that he fancies himself as an interrogator and loves to show off. If only he could be induced to take his job more seriously and think less about himself and the effect he's making on other people, he might develop into a fairly efficient detective officer. Imagine if Bigot had been turned on to this job of yours. He would have swanked in that café to such an extent that he would have had everyone laughing at his antics, and those three rascals wouldn't have touched him with a barge-pole."

"You may be right," said Cooper, "but I'm thankful I haven't got to work under him as Verneuil has. I wonder why those two swindlers have got a prize-fighter working with them? Where does he come in?"

"Well, there are always moneyed folk about the prize ring. He may be a decoy for some rich patron of the noble art."

"He doesn't look as if he had the brains for acting as a decoy. I should have thought it more likely that he is kept in reserve for any rough work that may be wanted. Neither Polowski nor Zizon would be much good in a fight."

"No, but if the prize-fighter had been brought into Everett's flat to tackle him—and remember, Everett was a young man who could use his fists—the prize-fighter wouldn't have taken a knife to him or had a rough and tumble on the carpet. He would have landed him one on the point of the jaw and put him to sleep. The murderer must have been a smaller man than Everett, and that is why he used the knife."

Chapter Fourteen

THE RAILWAY official posted at the barrier in the Gare St. Lazare knew Brigadier Verneuil; he had also served his time in the French navy, and the freemasonry of the sea was a bond between them. They shook hands.

"Going down on a job?" asked the railwayman. "As you are travelling without a ticket you must be."

Verneuil's only reply was a wink. He made towards a second-class coach.

It would have been amusing to know what was passing through his mind as he sat at the back of the railway carriage, mechanically scrutinizing the other travellers boarding the train; but the thoughts that were causing the lines of amusement in his face had nothing to do with his fellow-travellers. He was thinking of his British *camarades* and their strange way of proceeding about their work. If we French police, he thought, were restrained from interrogating prisoners the prisons would be empty. It was bad enough to have judges and advocates and juries weeping over the rascals brought before them, and bringing all the skill and industry of detective officers to nought. In England, these Britishers had assured him, the police could count upon the goodwill of the public; in England a murderer was brought to justice and hanged in under three months from the date of his crime. Here in France people had forgotten how to punish; in fact a criminal had a career before him; he might end as a deputy if he pulled the right strings; and if he were a freemason he might attain to a Minister's portfolio. Well, well, it was a strange world and politics a dirty profession, but what was a police brigadier to do? He could not set the world right. Nevertheless, he wished that he had his British colleagues with him that evening. He was not daunted by the task that lay before him, nor did he, like Bigot, want an audience for the part he was to play, but numbers gave support to a man when he was engaged in a delicate investigation. To Verneuil all his investigations were delicate.

The coach was rapidly emptying; at Croissy he was the only passenger left in the vehicle. The sun had set and it was growing dark. Five minutes later the train pulled up at the station of le Pecq, and he discovered that he was the only passenger to alight on the platform.

Knowing his way he lost no time in reaching Pinet's little villa. He rang the bell. Instantly a light that had been showing through a chink in the shutters of the kitchen was extinguished. No one answered the bell, but electric light does not turn itself off automatically. Verneuil, though getting on in years, had been trained in the navy to make light of obstacles. He made light of Pinet's gate by vaulting over it. He made light of his lack of courtesy in taking no notice of the bell, by running up the steps and kicking at Pinet's front door. Almost he hoped that Pinet or his platinum blonde lady would telephone to the local police at Croissy, for then there would be an amusing complication that would fly all over the village, losing nothing in the telling. But Pinet knew that too, and footsteps were heard approaching the front door.

"Who is it?" asked an anxious voice.

"The police," proclaimed Verneuil in decisive tones. "Open the door."

Very reluctantly bolts were slipped back, the door opened a few inches and Pinet's face appeared.

"You remember me, monsieur—a brigadier from the ninth *arrondissement* in Paris. I called on you a day or two ago."

Pinet switched on the light and opened the door. "Come in, monsieur," he said, leading the way into the dining-room.

"Shall we sit down, monsieur?" said Verneuil. "I have a few additional questions to ask you. I am told that you received a visit from three gentlemen on Friday evening."

Pinet looked at him blankly and shook his head. "You have been misinformed, monsieur."

Verneuil screwed up his eyes in a sceptical smile. "You must jog your memory, monsieur. On Friday evening, soon after it grew dark, three gentlemen from Paris rang your gate bell and were admitted."

"Oh! I see what you mean. Many people—com-mission agents and commercial travellers—call on us who live in le Pecq to see things, and it is the practice here to admit them to show a sample of their goods. Some men did call last week."

"What were they selling? Do you remember?"

"Gramophone records, I think it was."

"You must do more thinking than that, monsieur. Indeed, it must not be thinking, it must be sober fact. I put the question to you. What did these gentlemen come here for?"

"They were working the whole district, selling gramophone records."

"Ah! Working the whole district, were they? And if I told you that they came straight from the train to this house and went back from this house to the station you would be surprised to hear it? Come, come, monsieur. This is no time for fooling. I want a straight answer to a straight question. What was the object of their visit?"

Pinet rose from his chair and began to pace the floor.

"Well, monsieur, as you seem to know so much I had better tell you the truth. They wanted me to buy some gold."

"But why should they think that you were in a financial position to buy gold—you, a struggling journalist—unless they thought that you knew of people rich enough to become purchasers?"

"Yes, that was it," assented Pinet eagerly. "They wanted me to supply them with names and addresses of speculating people."

"I see. They called on you as a journalist. Perhaps they called on other gentlemen connected with the Press—that Englishman who was murdered, for example. They might have called on him."

"They did; he told me so."

"M. Everett told you so? When?"

"When I called upon him on the Tuesday evening."

"What did he say?"

"He asked me whether I had had a visit from three foreigners who were selling gold; that they had called upon him, and he had told them plainly that he knew of no one who would speculate in gold, and that they had gone slowly down the stairs discussing something in a foreign language. He said he did not like the looks of the men."

"Would you be prepared to identify them?"

"Well, monsieur, I saw them in a rather poor light." He pointed towards the electric bulb and assumed a confidential manner. "You must remember, monsieur, that this is a very lonely place, and there is very little police protection in the neighbourhood. When I told these men that I could not do what they wanted, they assumed a threatening manner, and I was in two minds about telephoning to the police. I should not care to identify them unless they were safely under lock and key."

"You realize, monsieur, that all the statements you have made to me this afternoon can be put to the test, and if any of them prove to be false…"

"Of course I know that. If I've been lying to you I should deserve punishment. You can test my statements as much as you like; you will find them all true, though, of course, I cannot answer for the truth of what others have told me; but when M. Everett said that the men had called upon him I believed him, because he had no motive in lying."

Verneuil's face as he screwed up his eyes whimsically was a picture. "But you, monsieur, you had a motive when you told me at first that these men had called at your house to sell you gramophone records. That, at any rate, was untrue."

"Well, monsieur, you must put yourself in my place. Those three men are dangerous. I fenced with you at first because I am afraid of them. If they get to know that I have told you the real object of their visit, my life may not be safe. At any rate I have now told the truth."

There was a long silence. Verneuil was none of your heaven-born cross-examiners, but he was a shrewd judge of character. "We did not start our conversation very well, monsieur, did we? For example, that gramophone record story… One fact remains unexplained. Why should they have selected you out of all the people living in the district of Seine-et-Oise as a person likely to buy gold, or even to indicate any other person as a likely purchaser. No, monsieur, you will have to give me a better explanation than that. If you had said that your late uncle had left you a fortune, for example, and I had believed it, well… then I might have gone away feeling more satisfied than I am."

He saw the pallor of fear showing in Pinet's face, and, rather than frighten him into taking to his heels, he continued, "But you assure me that you have now told me the actual truth, and, being a man of honour as you appear to be, I must accept your assurance. I will not detain you further, monsieur. *Bonsoir et bonne nuit.*"

He allowed Pinet to bow him out of the house. On the way back to Paris he found himself alone in the second-class coach. He was not altogether pleased with the result of his interrogation, but in going over it in his mind he came to the conclusion that he had done well not to frighten Pinet too much. From St. Lazare station he made straight for Richardson's hotel, and related to him, as far as his memory served, Pinet's answers to his questions.

Richardson heard him to the end. "What impression did he make upon you?" he asked.

"When a man begins by telling you a lie and then confesses what he declares to be the truth, monsieur, you draw a certain conclusion, is it not so? My impression is that this M. Pinet had something to hide when he told me that those three foreigners had come to sell him gramophone records, and his excuse for that lie did not ring true. To my belief he has joined the little gang and is sharing in the profits. In thinking over what he told me I came to the conclusion that the men had approached M. Everett, but that he, unlike Pinet, had refused to have anything to do with them."

"And then?"

"And then he knew their secret, and thus he was a source of danger to them. What more natural than that they should pick a quarrel with him and—" Verneuil shrugged his shoulders expressively.

"And killed him, you mean?"

"Men of that type, monsieur, believe in the adage, 'Dead men tell no tales.' But when we get them to the police station..."

"You mean to arrest them, then?"

"I shall have to get the permission of M. Bigot before I do that. I shall see him to-morrow morning and tell him the result of our inquiries."

"At what hour to-morrow will you see him?"

"At ten o'clock, and I should like you, monsieur, to come with me to his room. You will be a support to me."

Richardson thought for a moment. In reality he was not for rushing matters, having still some hope that Cooper would obtain some useful admission from the men, but, as another interview with Bigot might produce some new fact, he promised to be at the police station at ten, and Verneuil took his leave.

Richardson went to the telephone and rang up the Grand Hotel, asking to be put through to M. Rivaux. "Is that you, Cooper? Richardson speaking. V.—you know who I mean—has just got back. It's too long a story to tell you over the phone. I'll come round."

The people at the Grand Hotel had come to know Richardson. Had they been of the inquisitive breed they might have thought it strange that a French Canadian should have as an intimate an Englishman of wealth and importance, for so they considered Richardson, but hotel people in Paris have long lost all curiosity about the strange guests that they harbour under their roof. Richardson was shown up to Room 33 without any circumlocution.

"Well?" inquired Cooper. "What did Verneuil get out of our friend at le Pecq?"

"Precious little, if you ask me. Pinet began by saying that those three rascals were peddling gramophone records from house to house. That was too much for Verneuil to swallow, and so he told Pinet, but our friend Verneuil is no born cross-examiner. Pinet went to the length of saying that the men had gold to sell, and they wanted the addresses of people with money enough to buy it. According to Verneuil's account of his interrogation,

Pinet's statement that the men had come to him because he was a journalist had been put into his mouth by Verneuil himself. The statement that those rascals had called on Everett as well as Pinet, and that Everett told him so, was also unconsciously suggested by Verneuil's questions, I believe."

"As an interrogator poor old Verneuil seems to be a dud."

"Yes, but the interview is going to have one important result—he wants to bring those three men down to the police station and turn them inside out if Bigot will let him. Apparently he dare not do it on his own."

"Won't that queer our pitch? I mean, won't it break off all relations between Polowski and me?"

"It will, but you never can tell with the French police how far they will get if they start running the harrow over a set of suspects. That Roumanian Jew, for instance... It wouldn't take much to make him squeal."

"Oh, Lord!" sighed Cooper. "We don't seem to be getting along very fast, do we?"

"Come, this is no time for pessimism. This is the first time we've had a glimmer of a motive for the crime, and Verneuil has asked me to be present when he beards his chief, M. Bigot. That will be all to the good. And now let me tell you of a little adventure that I had this afternoon. When I left you I went for a walk down the rue de la Paix and into the Place Vendôme. You remember we went there together for our second day in Paris? In the late afternoon the Place is a favourite parking-place for cars: there are rows of them on either side of the Vendôme column. I was just beginning to take a short cut across the Place when a taxi pulled up a few yards in front of me, and a lady got out of it. There was something familiar about her; she had platinum blonde hair—that's common enough in Paris, as you know—but there was something that struck me about her walk when she had paid off her taxi. She had the same slight limp that

Pinet's young woman had; I couldn't be mistaken. Well, I hung about to see where she went. She did not notice me. She went straight to a very swish car—the newest streamline model—and taking a key from her bag she unlocked it, started the engine and drove off alone.

"I asked Verneuil if she was there when he called, and he said no. So the lady can run to a new car. She drives it up to Paris, parks it, and goes off in a taxi to a destination unknown. There's something in this that does not meet the eye."

"Yes, it looks as if Pinet had joined up with the gang—a poor journalist would scarcely run to a car of that kind. She's worth watching."

"She is, but I don't trust the ordinary French policeman to keep on her track without giving himself away."

"Couldn't I do it? It would give me some occupation for to-morrow."

"How could you do it? In that hat of yours? You'd be spotted a mile off, and you can't go in your own clothes, because you might run across some member of the gang."

"Well, then, what about that policewoman who came with me to the Café Veil? She could do it all right."

"She might, but I think of doing it myself. You can do the sights of Paris to-morrow, and I'll come round after lunch to tell you how we got on with friend Bigot."

Chapter Fifteen

WHEN RICHARDSON arrived at the police station of the ninth *arrondissement*, he found Verneuil awaiting him with some impatience.

"M. Bigot knows nothing about the subject of our visit to him as yet; it will be a surprise. If you'll give yourself the trouble of coming straight to his room I will do the necessary talking."

He tapped at Bigot's door and threw it open, ushering in his British colleague. On seeing Richardson, Bigot jumped to his feet and shook hands. He was in an expansive mood that morning. "Ah! Monsieur Richardson, I am glad to see you again, though of necessity you will not have much to tell me."

Richardson looked to Verneuil to open the proceedings.

"On the contrary, Monsieur Richardson has a good deal to tell you. He has desired me to make his report to you since he does not altogether trust his French."

Thereupon Verneuil told Bigot what the reader already knows about the gang which was selling bogus Russian gold, and about its connection with Pinet and the attempt to victimize Sergeant Cooper, who was playing the part of a rich young Canadian.

When the story was told to the end, Bigot burst into a shout of laughter. Mastering his mirth he turned to Richardson. "Please excuse me, monsieur, but the joke, you will agree, is irresistible, when I tell you that I am on the eve of clearing up the mystery of the assassination of Mr. Everett. I have forborne to make a report to His Excellency the Ambassador until my evidence is complete. In so delicate an inquiry one must be allowed time—is it not so with you in London?"

His manner was so convincing that Richardson inquired whether he had reached the stage of arresting a suspect, because, as he explained, there was now a question of arresting the three swindlers and subjecting them to close interrogation.

Bigot waved his hand in front of his face. "Not yet, my friends, not yet. Go on with your playacting a little longer. Let your young Canadian millionaire, who is known to me as Sergeant Cooper, fool them to the top of his bent—it can do no harm; indeed it may even be amusing. But an arrest at this moment would be a serious matter. It could not be kept from reporters, and the publicity would entirely spoil my *coup*. I expect information from the Lobby of the Chamber this very evening. The *coup* will be theatrical in the sensation that it will produce."

After that there seemed nothing more to be said. Verneuil opened the door and followed Richardson out.

"This way, monsieur," he said, steering the Englishman to the room in which he had previously worked. As usual it was unoccupied; scraps of written paper were scattered over the table; one of the cupboards was open, disclosing thick piles of papers discoloured with age and dirt; there seemed to be no system.

"You see how it is, comrade," said Verneuil, jerking his thumb towards his chief's room; "working his promotion, that is his present preoccupation. To him it matters not whether he finds the guilty person or not, provided that it makes a public sensation and that the newspapers refer to Bigot as 'that astute *commissaire*.'"

"But I should have thought that in the line he is taking he must be making enemies as well as friends. Is he not fishing in troubled waters when he goes to the Lobby of the Chamber for information?"

"You have said it, comrade. How many police officers have I seen fall through the politicians and their newspapers, and when they are given the key of the fields they can count upon no one to befriend them. You will see what will happen with M. Bigot."

"I hope, monsieur, that this will not disturb our pleasant relations; that we can still continue to work together."

"Yes, monsieur, but I must confess to you that this refusal to let me arrest that little gang of three has been a shock to me. I say to myself, 'What more can we do? The case will have to join those thousands of dossiers which are treated as waste-paper.'"

"I see no reason for discouragement at this stage," said Richardson. "If M. Bigot will not sanction an arrest, we must continue the investigation in our own way; for example, our Canadian millionaire may be able to do a little astute interrogation on his own account. There is another thing that might be done, monsieur; it is to have one more interview with the lady whom the Press called Mademoiselle X—Madame Blanchard. You have her address?"

"Certainly. I will take you there and you shall ask her any question you like. We might even go there this morning. What do you want her to tell you?"

"Whether she had ever heard M. Everett hint that he had been asked to join a syndicate for selling gold as M. Pinet told you."

"Very well—we will start at once."

A constable put his head in at the door. "A gentleman is asking to see a member of the police *judiciaire*. Will you see him, M. Verneuil? The chief is not in his room."

"Yes, show him in here." Richardson had risen. "No, you need not leave me to see him alone, monsieur; it is no doubt some trifling incident that he comes to report—the loss of a dog, perhaps."

He had hardly spoken when the door opened to admit a young man of under thirty, who seemed to be in a state of agitation. He presented his card on which was inscribed his name and address, "Dr. Albert Moreau, II bis rue Jean Bissot."

"I do not know whether I am doing right in coming to you, monsieur, but since you are the police officers of this quarter, you can at least advise me. Yesterday evening the *concierge* of a building in this neighbourhood telephoned to say that one of her tenants was very ill and would I come at once. I went to the house and was taken upstairs to a room where a woman of between thirty and forty was lying groaning on a bed."

"What class of woman?" asked Verneuil.

"Oh, she may have been a street prostitute; she told me that she was a seamstress out of work. I examined her and questioned her; she had vomited more than once and this had left her weak and suffering. In fact, all the symptoms pointed to poisoning."

"You mean that it was a case of attempted murder?"

"No, monsieur, that was not my impression. She denied the suggestion that she could be suffering from poisoning, but the symptoms were entirely those of irritant poison, and her manner when I questioned her was strange. While I was talking to her I made a cursory inspection of the cupboard, but I could see no bottle in it. My impression remains that it was a case of attempted suicide, and that is why I have come to you. Now that I have done my duty I must leave you; I have patients to see."

"You have not yet given me the woman's name and address."

"Ah! Did I not? It was Thérèse Volny, and her address is 100 rue Vidal."

The doctor bowed himself out with little ceremony.

"The address is quite close to that of Madame Blanchard, monsieur. We might do the two inquiries this morning; that is if you care to see how we work on a case like that described to us by the doctor."

Richardson considered. He had nothing particular to do before lunch, and he did want to see "Mademoiselle X" to ask her a specific question, but the other case—the attempted suicide—had no interest for him. Nevertheless he fell in with Verneuil's suggestion. Their first visit was to the house in the rue Vidal, an old house in which generations of Parisians had lived and died. The staircase was narrow, the planking worn, the wallpaper torn and stained; the very air they breathed as they entered was fetid. They found the *concierge* in a little den constructed behind and under the staircase. A visit from a police officer in plain clothes was an event in her squalid life; she was bursting with importance.

"Ah, monsieur, I expected this. The doctor who attended the lady upstairs is young and impressionable. What might be considered by us as an ordinary occurrence seemed to him something terrible."

"Tell me exactly what happened."

"Well, monsieur, last night Madame Volny entered this office looking dreadful. She was staggering; she had to cling to that railing to hold herself erect. I thought, of course, that it was the old story; that she had drunk more than was good for her, for I will not disguise from you, monsieur, that the habit of the bottle has been growing upon her. She said, 'This time I think I am going to die; my legs are too weak to get me up the stairs.' So I helped her up. Scarcely had I got her on to the bed, monsieur, than she was sick, and the sickness was so grave that I telephoned to the doctor. It did not seem to be only the sickness of a drunken person; and when the doctor came he said that she had been poisoned."

"Has she ever threatened to take her own life?"

"No, monsieur, and she is not one to do that. She's of a cheerful temperament and takes the ups and downs of women of her class with resignation—up one day and down the next."

"Did she tell you where she had been last night?"

"No, monsieur, to say truth, I never asked her. She makes the round of the cafés every night, I believe."

"She may have had some stroke of ill fortune."

"I think not, monsieur, and I'll tell you why. When I was getting her to bed last night, and slipping off her blouse, a little bundle fell out. 'Give me that,' she cried eagerly. I did. Monsieur, you may believe me or you may not, it was a roll of notes of one hundred francs tied up into a packet. There must have been a hundred of them."

"Ah! Then it wasn't a moment for suicide. She must have found a generous patron. If you will show me the way we will have a word with her."

Led by the woman, the two men climbed the squalid stairs to the third floor. Using her master-key, the *concierge* called, "Thérèse, here are two gentlemen to see you." A faint voice from an inner room replied, "Tell them I'm ill; tell them I'm in bed. I can see no one."

"Follow me, messieurs; I'll take you into her room."

The flat itself was a surprise. The furniture, picked up no doubt in sale-rooms, was a mingling of many periods, but though the taste that mingled them was vulgar, the things themselves were good of their kind. The floors were carpeted with oriental rugs. The bedroom into which the two police officers were ushered was unexpectedly tidy. Clothes had been put away in a wardrobe and drawers; there was a *cabinet de toilette* screened off from the bedroom, and on the bed lay the woman they had come to see. It was not a moment when such a woman could look her best; her face was lined, puffy and yellow; her eyes suffused; she was only just beginning to recover from her sickness overnight.

"But who are these gentlemen?" she asked indignantly.

The *concierge* whispered in her ear the reason for the intrusion. She sank back on her pillows, resigned.

"I have to ask you a few questions, madame?" began Verneuil. "You are Thérèse Volny? What is your occupation? A seamstress out of work?"

She inclined her head and began to talk volubly.

"Messieurs, you have been sent here to waste your time on a false errand. That young doctor was mistaken. He thinks that I am suffering from poison. It is nothing of the kind. I will keep no secrets from you. For some days I have been imprudent in drinking. The habit reached its climax last night. If my stomach was poisoned as the doctor thinks, it was poisoned solely by alcohol. I have been a fool."

"You have been taking remedies?"

"Drugs, you mean? No, that is not one of my vices. I never touch drugs."

"Where was it that you were drinking last night?"

Lines of obstinacy formed about her mouth. "I do not remember, monsieur."

"I ask you only for the name of the last café that you frequented."

"And I tell you, monsieur, that I do not remember."

"Then if you do not remember the café, tell me who paid for the liquor you drank?"

"I paid for it myself. I spent the evening alone."

"But the money you brought home—several thousand francs?"

"Oh, that money? It was given to me days ago by a foreigner who was about to leave Paris."

"His name?"

"He did not tell me his name, nor his nationality, nor where he was going."

During this conversation Richardson had to keep reminding himself that this was not one of his cases, otherwise he would be making a thorough search of the flat. Almost involuntarily he took a step towards the *cabinet de toilette* to look for bottles, when the woman's yellow face flushed and she cried, "Why does your friend go looking into my private affairs? Surely a lady's *toilette* is exempt from police prying!"

Richardson explained rather lamely that he was looking to see what medicine the doctor had prescribed for her.

The *concierge* had knelt down beside the bed to hold a whispered conversation with the patient. Verneuil drew Richardson into the outer room to discuss the case.

"Listen, my friend, it seems to me that we are wasting our time here. The woman herself laughs at the idea of poisoning and she must know best. She ascribes her sickness to drink, and there again she must know best. That it was not an attempt at suicide is evident from the fact that she carried a considerable sum of money on her person. The wonder is that she was not robbed of it. What say you? I will admonish her about her drinking and her way of life, and then we'll go on to the rue Chapelle."

Richardson agreed, but suggested that the roll of notes should be produced for their inspection.

"She'll fight over that," objected Verneuil, "but I think we ought to see them. I'll see what I can do by persuasion."

He went back to the bedroom. Richardson remained near the open door; he was curious to see what Verneuil's idea of friendly persuasion might be.

The courtliness of the lower deck peeped out in Verneuil's "friendly" admonition. "Listen," he said to the sufferer. "If you go on drinking like this you will go down those stairs feet first. Give it up, I say. If drink you must have, let it be a *limonade*, or a Vichy; that will not harm the stomach of a mosquito. At the rate you are going you will be dead before the year's out."

The poor woman burst into tears and began to sob. The success of Verneuil's address seemed to gratify him. He laid his huge paw on her shoulder and patted her in paternal fashion. "Now, my little one, let me have a look at that money you brought home. Where did you put it?"

Thérèse redoubled her sobs, but made no other sign that she had heard him.

"Come!" he said, "you heard my question. Where did you put that money?"

"It's under her pillow, *monsieur le commissaire*," whispered the *concierge.*

There seemed to Richardson's ears to be a physical struggle, for the sick woman screamed and Verneuil returned to the sitting-room with a fat bundle of hundred-franc notes. "Help me to count these, comrade. The amount should be given in my report." He unfastened the bundle. The count amounted to a round sum of five thousand francs, but the fact that struck Richardson was that the bundle was tied with a black and white shoe-lace. He called Verneuil's attention to this; he went to the door and beckoned to the *concierge*.

"Have you ever seen Madame Volny wear shoes with this sort of lace in them?"

The woman shook her head emphatically. "Never, monsieur."

Verneuil went back to the bedroom with the bundle of notes tied up with the same shoe-lace and restored it to its owner. "When you come to count the notes," he said, "you will find the count exact. It is not my habit to make any charge for my visit." With a final fatherly pat on her shoulder he took his leave.

As they descended the stairs he said, "We have wasted a good hour, comrade. It's your turn now with Madame Blanchard."

Chapter Sixteen

WHEN THE two police officers were in the street heading towards the rue Chapelle, Verneuil delivered himself of a monologue on the duties of Paris policemen.

"I said just now, comrade, that we had wasted our time, but on reflection I feel that I was wrong. Certainly it is no business of ours to concern ourselves with the doings of these women, provided that they keep within the law, but a police officer with a conscience may drop words of admonition that stick in the minds of these poor creatures. For, look you, they are superstitious; they believe in omens and fortune-tellers; any charlatan can impress them, and therefore good advice tendered without seeking any return must appeal to them."

"You believed her story about drink being the cause of her illness?"

"With a woman like that, what does it matter whether her story be true or false? She drinks—yes —you can see that in her face. And for her morals, they are no concern of ours, but rather of the *curé*. As for suicide, the world would not be either better or worse if she were out of it. Yet why should a woman with five thousand francs in her pocket want to leave the world before it was spent?"

"You think that the doctor was wrong in his diagnosis?"

"Yes, that's what I think. You, comrade, are a man after my own heart. Your reasoning is sound; you do not run about seeking for commendation from those above you, nor pushing your way into the *couloirs* of the Chamber in search of sensation. No. You, like myself, try to establish the truth without fear and without favour."

They had turned into the rue Chapelle and made for Number 8. From the *concierge* they learned that Madame Blanchard was lodging with her parents, Monsieur and Madame Cogny, on the first floor; Madame Blanchard went up to their flat only ten minutes before. It was the door on the left of the lift on the second floor.

A little *bonne* answered the door bell. "Yes, messieurs; Madame Blanchard is at home. What name shall I give?"

Verneuil took out a well-thumbed visiting-card and said that he would not *déranger* either Monsieur or Madame Cogny if he could have a few words with Madame Blanchard.

While the maid retired to her mistress, they stood their ground in the little entrance hall. "You, comrade, will do the questioning here. I will be at hand as your interpreter." He had scarce spoken when Madame Blanchard fluttered in, her quick-coming breath betraying her apprehensions. Verneuil set clumsily to work to restore her composure.

"Good morning, madame; you have already met my friend from the British Embassy. He wishes to put to you a few questions which will not be difficult for you to answer."

"Will you give yourselves the trouble to come into the *salon*, messieurs; there we can sit down."

She conducted them into a miniature drawing-room, furnished with good taste, and drew up chairs for them.

"I shall not detain you long, madame," said Richardson in his halting French. "My first question is whether Mr. Everett at any time led you to suppose that he would shortly have money, either by inheritance or through some business that had been offered to him."

The young woman knit her brow, thinking. "We talked of so many things, monsieur. I do not remember hearing him say that he would be rich. Stay, I do remember now, that, on one occasion, when we talked about going on a holiday to Italy, he said, 'It may be sooner than you think. I, too, want to visit Italy, and as soon as I have secured the money for our journey I shall ask you to come with me.'"

"Secured the money? What did you understand by that?"

"I did not ask him what he meant. I thought that perhaps money was owing to him in his own country, or again, that it had been left to him by some relative."

"He spoke of it as a certainty?"

"No, monsieur, rather as a possibility. I felt that it would be indelicate to question him. I preferred to wait until he told me plainly what he meant."

"Did he ever tell you that three foreigners had been trying to induce him to join them in a speculation?"

"Three foreigners? No, monsieur; if he had told me that I am sure I should have remembered it."

Richardson rose as an intimation that he had come to the end of his questions, but Verneuil was not disposed to let her off quite so easily.

"You've had no journalists to see you, I hope, madame?"

The young woman flushed and replied readily, "No, monsieur, and I hope that now there will not be any." She hesitated, and then in a tremulous voice asked them whether they were likely to trace the murderer.

"Not yet, madame, but I will not hide from you that we are pursuing lines of inquiry which may at any moment result in an arrest."

Richardson left the flat feeling haunted by the tragic eyes of this young married woman who had buried her heart in Père la Chaise, and had a life before her with a man she could not love.

"One has to eat, M. Verneuil," he said. "Will you become my guest at the Restaurant des Gourmets which M. Bigot discovered for us? If we talk 'shop' no one can find fault with us."

Verneuil accepted with enthusiasm; it seemed that the viands of such an establishment did not come his way very often.

"I suppose," said Richardson, when they had given their order, "that you are not feeling optimistic about this case of ours?"

"One never knows how a case may turn out," mumbled Verneuil as he munched his beefsteak.

"Certainly one never knows. I wake in the night sometimes, feeling that I am on the verge of a discovery," said Richardson.

"You will forgive me for saying that when once your head has touched the pillow you should dismiss all thoughts of your cases. That is a golden rule which I have always followed."

"Whether I think of it at night or in the daytime, it all comes to the same—we are not getting on. I thought that something might come out of those Russian swindlers, who are trying to victimize my comrade Cooper, but even that is hanging fire."

"What will you, if my inspector will not sanction the arrest of those men? I would soon have got from them the real reason why they called on Pinet at le Pecq. Ah! Comrade, you should cultivate the optimism of our friend Bigot, who thinks, God pity him! that he is on the eve of bringing the crime home to the new Radical Minister of Education, M. Quesnay."

Richardson made no reply; an idea had occurred to him. "What are your duties this afternoon, M. Verneuil?"

"To sit in my office like a spider in wait for a fly."

"Because I was wondering whether something might turn up if we visited the Zoological Gardens in the Bois de Vincennes. M. Bigot told me that the film which we found in the dead man's rooms consisted of wild animals in cages, but he did not show it to me."

"I can show you something better than the film—the prints that were taken from it."

Verneuil dragged forth from his pocket a well-worn note-case and drew from it eight Kodak prints for Richardson to examine. They consisted of studies of lions, tigers, giraffes, bears and baboons, all marred as pictures by the intervening iron railings. They were clearly the work of an inexperienced amateur, for no trouble had been taken to take the subjects in a favourable light with the proper diaphragm and exposure.

"These prints have given me an idea, M. Verneuil. Why should we not go out there this afternoon? A conversation with the keepers might produce something new."

The generous wine which Verneuil had imbibed freely made it possible for him to agree to any proposal. He helped himself to another glass of it, and screwing up his eyes with a whimsical smile he said, "A very excellent suggestion!"

Regardless of expense, Richardson pronounced in favour of a taxi drive all the way, salving his conscience in the matter of petty cash by the reflection that it would not be the police fund that would have to pay for the jaunt, and that if they were to see the principal men they must not arrive at the gardens too late. His companion seemed disposed to sleep. This did not suit so keen a man as Richardson. He tapped the back of his knotted hand.

"Probably you know the principal men of the gardens, M. Verneuil? I should like to put a few questions to them."

Verneuil winked languidly. It was no affair of his and he was strongly inclined to a post-prandial nap; in fact his eyelids were unblushingly closed when they drew up at the entrance to the garden. Even when Richardson was paying their fare he was sleeping as peacefully as an infant.

"We have arrived," bellowed Richardson, plucking at his sleeve and helping him out of the taxi.

Richardson found it curious to be the leader of the expedition, but he reflected that it was very good for his French. The man at the turnstile gave him clear directions to the superintendent's office. With his arm linked through that of Verneuil, Inspector Richardson found his way thither, and was informed that the superintendent was at that moment patrolling the gardens and would probably be found in or about the lion enclosure. There they found him, and Verneuil was by this time alert enough to present his British comrade.

The superintendent seemed young to be in that responsible position. He had learned his wild-beast lore in the French African colonies, and he was in such close touch with lions as to be able to enter their enclosure unarmed and single-handed to train them, but on this particular afternoon, as he explained, the lion standing royally facing the gate was in no mood for entertaining visitors and he had beaten a hasty retreat, locking the gate behind him. He was at pains to do the honours of his establishment to his visitors. These were, to take them into every part of the cages that were not open to the public; for example, behind every tier of cages ran a passage used by the keepers for cleaning the cages and providing their occupants with food. A miniature tramway ran along these passages, with trucks loaded with raw meat for the carnivora. Richardson became keenly interested. He asked Verneuil to lend him the photographs again. They had arrived at the wolves. Three of these animals were circling their cage persistently; it was a sign that dinner-time was near. A few adults and children could be seen standing on the opposite side of the cage where the light was strongest. Running through the prints Richardson slipped out one, evidently taken from this very spot, but the wolves had been full-fed and somnolent when the lens was snapped. He knew enough about photography to see that the hand which snapped the shutter had been that of a tyro, for no experienced Kodak fiend would have thought of taking a picture with the strong light facing the lens; indeed the photograph had been a very poor one.

The superintendent turned round to see why his guests had halted, and Richardson showed him the print.

"*Tiens!*" said the superintendent. "This must have been taken from this very spot."

"I suppose that no one but you brings people into this gallery?"

"According to my orders that is so, but I have little doubt that when I am otherwise engaged, some of my men usurp the privilege in the hope of earning *pourboires.*"

"Do you bring round visitors every day?"

"Oh, no, monsieur; I make the privilege as rare as I can. It is only distinguished visitors that are invited behind the cages, for example, deputies or members of the Press who are preparing articles for their paper."

"Ah!" interrupted Verneuil. "Deputies? M. Quesnay, for example?"

The superintendent laughed. "You seem to know a great deal about the gardens, *monsieur le commissaire*, but since you cite M. Quesnay, I admit that I took him round less than three weeks ago."

"And he took photographs?"

"He did, and very good they were. He sent me prints of them afterwards."

"What sort of a camera did he use?"

"Ah! That was the trouble. None of your Kodaks for that gentleman. He had a big studio camera, and the difficulty was how to get a firm stand for it when its lens was pushed through the bars. In the end we had to lend him a stool high enough to bring the camera well above the floor. You know, messieurs, one has to be careful whom one brings into this passage. Only the other day a journalist presented his card and I took him round. He was accompanied by a lady whom I supposed to be a person of good sense, but I caught her just in time thrusting her hand into the hyena's cage to stroke its neck. If the beast had once got his teeth into her hand she would have lost her arm, and there would have been a public outcry against me; I stopped her just in time. *Tiens!* That might have been the very person who took those photographs. I remember now that she had a camera with her, and that the journalist who brought her laughed at the way she was photographing everything against the light."

"Do you remember what kind of a woman she was?

The superintendent shook his head doubtfully. "I remember that she was tall and dressed like a *femme du monde*, with that dyed hair that fashionable women are now wearing—platinum blonde, I think they call it."

Richardson caught Verneuil's eye. "Do you remember the name of the journalist?"

The superintendent shook his head.

"Or the name of the paper he represented?"

"No, monsieur; so many journalists come here and show their cards that one confuses them."

Probably the superintendent had never conducted so absent-minded a couple round his garden. After all, since he was in too conspicuous a place to be tipped, the least that visitors could do was to appear interested. After their visit to the hyena's cage, where the lady with tinted hair had so nearly lost an arm, all three men, acting as if by common impulse, glanced at their watches. Each had remembered an engagement. They shook hands warmly; the two visitors even asked leave to come to the gardens again, but they parted on this occasion, it must be confessed, with relief.

The two police officers made for the nearest Metro station, discussing what they had heard as they went.

"It seems to me," said Richardson, "that wherever we go we run into that platinum blonde lady of Pinet's."

"Many ladies are platinum blondes in Paris just now; it has become the rage to tint their hair with chemicals."

"Yes, but a platinum blonde lady who photographs wolves from the passage behind the cages, and whose photographs are found lying undeveloped in the room of a murder; whose husband or protector swears that he has no camera of that particular size—it sets one thinking. One can understand his motive for lying when once he had denied possession of the camera, but—"

"If it comes to that," interrupted Verneuil, "what motive could Pinet have had for killing that young Englishman? Do you think it possible that it was the woman herself who used the dagger?"

"What motive could she have had? Then there's another mystery to clear up. Where did she get the money for buying that streamline car? It cost twenty-six thousand francs if it cost a *sou*."

"We shall have to keep an eye on that lady," said Verneuil grimly. "We must know about that camera and about that car. I shall pay another visit to le Pecq, and if I find it necessary, search the house from roof to basement."

"And I must leave you when we reach the Concorde. I have to visit my friend, who is becoming weary of his part as a Canadian millionaire."

Chapter Seventeen

M. Quesnay, the newly appointed Minister of Education, was the son of a lawyer in Marseilles, a little black-bearded man with a paunch, who had tried the law, and finding himself wanting in the qualities for success in that profession, had fallen back upon politics for a livelihood. It had taken him some time to decide which of the many political parties would suit him best, and which constituency he should stand for. Having no political convictions of his own he was inclined to join the Socialists, until he remembered that the Socialist deputy for Toulouse had once played him a scurvy trick during one of his appearances at the Bar, during a case in which they had both been briefed. Besides, the Socialists were cutting a sorry figure at the moment; whereas the Radicals were actually in power and seemed likely to remain so. He became a freemason.

In reality it mattered little what label he bore if he could persuade the electors that he was the kind of man who would serve their private interests. As to the constituency, what better than his mother's little town, where his grandfather still carried on his business as a cooper of wine-casks and was as highly respected as his reputed wealth deserved? He knew just enough about lobbying in the Chamber to lay plans for serving his electors. There was a rather ruinous bridge over a rivulet near the town which would cost them money to repair. Why should not the road be classed as a military road, and the charge for repairing it fall upon the military budget? Then the money that would have had to be spent upon the bridge could be diverted to the building of a cinema and dance hall which would add to the amenities of the town. He had burned the midnight oil in composing five speeches and committing them to memory. With very slight modification they would serve him on all occasions—electoral, presidential, patriotic. These he delivered before a mirror with the gestures appropriate to them, with his right leg slightly advanced, his chest thrown out, his eyes ready to roll in ecstasy when delivering what he imagined to be soul-stirring passages which hostile critics might have described as empty platitudes. For Jules Quesnay was no genius, though he had the keen sense of self-interest which is a major part of the equipment of professional politicians.

So Jules Quesnay was duly elected and went to live in a tiny flat in Paris, equipped with a telephone and little else that conduced to modern comfort. He was a full-blown member of the Radical Socialist majority. He could be counted upon by his parliamentary chiefs to back them up both in the Chamber and the Lobby on every occasion. He had breathed deeply the demoralizing atmosphere of that House, where, if one may believe the man in the street, the good of the country was the last consideration of most of its members; where the last quality expected from its members was disinterested concern for the public weal; where the first was personal profit and advancement at the cost of the public. The electors in Jules Quesnay's constituency were alleged to be as little concerned with the good of the State as their deputy himself; all that they asked from him was that he should contrive by foul means or fair to serve their interests at the expense of those of their neighbours; to intrigue for well-paid government posts for their sons and daughters and to relieve them from some of the burdens of taxation.

Jules Quesnay had not been doing at all badly. He had achieved the giddy height of an office in the Cabinet, albeit a modest one, but he had more than his share of the minor perquisites of a Government supporter—the membership of committees of inquiry, of sub-commissions of finances, of masonic reunions. He was not a hard worker, but to those who did not know him well he seemed indefatigable. Every evening he swaggered home with a swollen dispatch-case to get ready for the morrow's work. They did not know that it lay on the table untouched until the meeting next day, for Jules Quesnay had set before him as the first rule of life never to make an enemy, and as the second, never to be caught in doing anything that would lower his dignity as a rising politician. He did not know that the directors of his party policy spoke of him as *ce pauvre* Quesnay, which meant that he could be flattered into undertaking any disagreeable duty and be offered up as a sacrifice whenever things which he was connected with went wrong. In either case no protest from him was to be apprehended.

The story told about his adventure on February 6th had been perfectly true. Nature had been chary of her gifts to him at his birth; the gift of natural eloquence, of charm of manner— both very necessary to success in the calling which he had chosen—had been denied to him, and so had physical courage, but that form of human weakness, which no training can cure, may be concealed successfully in a civilized country except in moments of popular convulsion. It was hard that one of these should have occurred at the very moment when his efforts as a political *arriviste* promised to be crowned with success. There had been firing in the Place de la Concorde; the ex-soldiers had been trying to force the bridge towards the Chamber with the intention, so it was rumoured, of stringing up all the deputies they could find to the nearest lamp-posts. Small wonder that the Chamber had emptied itself miraculously, and that he was almost the only deputy left in it. On that fateful day the Chamber was no place for deputies; a thin blue line still held the bridge, but it was being forced backward, and then there would be nothing between these ravening wolves and the Chamber except an iron railing. An iron railing! What obstacle would this be to men who had stormed the German trenches! The Chamber was no place for him. One of the constables whose duty it was to be in attendance on the Chamber happened to pass through the Lobby. To him Jules Quesnay appealed and stammered out a request for information about the safest exit from the House. The policeman was dilatory of speech.

"Well, monsieur, some have taken the Metro; others have walked into the Boulevard St. Germain because they happen to live on this side of the Seine, but in your place I should take one of the auto-buses which are still running towards the Louvre. No one will molest an auto-bus."

Quesnay thanked him with tears in his eyes, and bolted out of the House along the Quai d'Orsay. The policeman had not deceived him; omnibuses were still running over the bridge in both directions, their engines drowning the noise of pistols and machine-guns less than a quarter of a mile away. The deputy had taken no account of the direction in which the motor-buses were running. He boarded the first that he saw, and it was not until after they had crossed the bridge that he realized that it had turned along the Quai in the direction of the rioting. Well, there was nothing to distinguish him from any other occupant of the vehicle; he wore no uniform or badge; he was naturally an inconspicuous figure at whom no one would look twice; he would risk it. But the sound of those machine-guns rattling on the bridge would, he knew, remain with him all his life.

Who had been the first to recognize him as a deputy will never be known. It must have been some brute who took an unhealthy interest in deputies and was suddenly seized by a vision of how comely Jules Quesnay would look, spinning round at the end of his rope with his tongue protruding from his bearded lips, who first began pointing when the auto-bus was held up at the bottom of the rue Royale. And when once a finger had been so pointed things began to happen. Fierce-looking ex-soldiers, infuriated by the carnage on the bridge, leapt on to the footboard. The conductor made a brave attempt to protect his passengers; women screamed. While the conductor was struggling with the invaders, Quesnay spied an avenue of escape. He could slip past the conductor, vault over the railing at the back, and make a bolt across the street to the Café Moreau. He did his leap unnoticed, and then members of the wolf-pack who were coming up caught sight of him and ran baying at his heels. The café had been converted into an impromptu field hospital; stretchers carrying wounded men were streaming into it; their presence must deter his pursuers. He darted in; wound his way between the stretchers into the lavatory and locked himself in. He could hear the shouts of the men who were searching for him; if they broke the lock and dragged him out he knew that he would be speechless from fear; none of the five set speeches which he had learned by heart would apply to this emergency. It would be the lamp-post for him, and in his end, dangling from the centre post facing the Faubourg St. Honoré, he would be a more conspicuous figure than he had ever been during his lifetime.

How long he stood behind that locked door he never knew. Hours seemed to have passed as he listened to the distant firing and the shouting in the streets, but his pursuers seemed to have melted away from the door, perhaps in pursuit of other victims. At any rate it was long before he dared withdraw the bolt and venture through the lines of stretchers into the street, where he hoped to be mistaken for one of the doctors.

Many things happen in Paris that pass unnoticed. Why should this innocuous adventure of his be dragged into the light by an Englishman who happened to have been an eye-witness? There was but one method of restoring his reputation for personal courage, and this was the chivalric method of challenging his detractor to a duel. He had never yet fought a duel, but his friend, M. Bernardeau, assured him that a lesson or two in a fencing school would fit him to pass through the ordeal with credit, and that as to personal risk of injury, the terms of the challenge could be so worded that at the first scratch which drew blood, the umpire would declare that honour was satisfied and the duel would be called off. So the challenge had been sent. Who could have foreseen that this Englishman would have refused to treat such a formal ceremony seriously, and should talk derisively of fighting him, Jules Quesnay, with his fists? Well, he had done what honour required of him and that was the end of a distasteful business as far as he was concerned.

This seemed destined to be an ill-fated year for him. Within the last few days his friend Bernardeau had stopped him in the Lobby of the Chamber and had said jocularly, "What have you been up to, my friend? There's a *flic* on your track."

"What do you mean?"

"He said he belonged to the ninth *arrondissement* and had been to the Zoological Gardens at Vincennes; and something about some photographs you've been taking."

"Photographs?" As much as could be seen of Quesnay's face seemed to turn livid; his friend noticed it.

"There's nothing to be alarmed about, I suppose. Probably he'll come down to see you again, and then you can get him to explain himself."

"If he comes again, I shall decline to see him. By what right does a *flic* enter the Chamber to question a Minister? How are we to discharge our duties according to our oaths if every *flic* in Paris is free to come in and submit us to an interrogatory? It is scandalous."

"Calm yourself, my friend; this *flic* may be pursuing some miscreant, and every citizen ought to assist him if he can. Besides, didn't I see in the papers that you were taking a pack of children to the Gardens and photographing them with a number of strange beasts? There was a Press photographer there who photographed you holding up a little one to bestow a cake upon a camel. It was a moving picture and the tears ran down my cheeks when I saw it."

But Quesnay did not recover his composure. He was still protesting under his breath when his friend left him.

And then a day later another deputy stopped him in the Lobby. "You'll soon be in the limelight, my dear fellow."

"What do you mean?"

"Only that a *flic* of my acquaintance—his name is Bigot—seems to be very much interested in your doings."

"Pshaw! About my taking photographs at the Zoological Gardens."

"He said nothing about photographs. He asked me about that duel of yours with that Englishman who was found dead in his flat."

"That is very ancient history."

"Yes, but he asked me a good deal about your movements during the last few weeks, and why you were interesting yourself in teaching zoology to children."

The deputy was surprised to notice that this last remark had a startling effect upon the composure of Quesnay, who swallowed once or twice before he replied, "That *flic* will have to be brought to order by his superiors. I don't know what he means."

"Hadn't you better see the man and have done with it?"

"Certainly not. It would only encourage him to come and annoy other deputies. These *flics* are only promoted constables and we must keep them in their places."

And then came the day when Quesnay found for the first time that he was being followed by a policeman in plain clothes. He was skirting the Place de la Concorde on the way home when he first became aware of it. Looking round for a taxi he had seen the man stop, and when he resumed his walk the policeman, as he took him to be, did the same. Without looking round he opened his watch-case and used the inside of the flap as a mirror. Yes, there was no doubt of it, for when he stopped the man did the same, just as he had done farther back. He was obviously a detective, a well-built man of between thirty and forty, clean-shaven and of a fresh complexion—a Norman or a Breton he took him to be. Quesnay resumed his walk, debating in his mind whether he should shake the man off or turn and ask him what he wanted. It required some courage, but anything was better than this continual sense of being under suspicion. He walked along the pavement beside the Tuileries Gardens for a good two hundred yards before bringing his courage to the sticking-point. The pavement was almost deserted when his mind was made up; he turned and began to walk firmly back to his tormentor. He lifted his hat.

"You have been following me for some time, monsieur, as if you desired to speak to me. I am the Minister, Jules Quesnay."

Bigot also swept off his hat, saying, "I am flattered at meeting so distinguished a man. I have been seeking an opportunity for an interview with you, but I was told that you are difficult of access. After all, every man who has achieved the honour of a Minister's portfolio is perforce difficult to approach. Shall we stop at that café over there and converse? It is a quiet place."

"No, monsieur, if we are to talk I prefer to take you to my apartment in the rue de Genes. We will take a taxi. Of course it is understood that our interview will in no way be an interrogatory. That would be an indignity to which I could not submit."

"I agree with you entirely, *monsieur le Ministre*. It is I who will submit myself to an interrogatory by you."

The remainder of the drive to the upper end of the rue de Gènes, bordering on the railway, was pursued in a constrained silence. Quesnay left Bigot to settle with the taxi-driver and led the way upstairs. The block of flats did not run to a lift. It was a mean little flat to which Bigot was admitted. He waited standing until this little southern deputy motioned him to a chair.

"Now, monsieur, I am ready to hear your explanation. Why have you been questioning people about me?"

Chapter Eighteen

BIGOT ADOPTED the manner which he had always found most successful in opening his interrogations—the polite, disarming manner. "That is very easy to explain, *monsieur le ministre*. It was thought that you would be in the position of being able to give us some useful information. It was not considered proper to approach you directly at this stage, and for that reason a few indirect inquiries were made."

"But what is it all about? What information do you think that I can give?"

"You have a perfect right to ask that, monsieur. Had anyone else put that question to me I might have fenced with it, but to a man of your high character and importance I will be perfectly frank. What we desire to know from you is what you were doing on the night of October 6th."

The effect of this question on Jules Quesnay was startling. His mouth fell open; his hands began to work; his breath came in gasps. Bigot took keen note of his disarray, but made no sign that he did so. There was silence for a few moments while the little man was pulling himself together. At last he found his voice.

"On the night of October 6th? How can anybody remember offhand what he was doing on a particular night two or three weeks ago? I should have to look in my diary."

"If the information that has reached us is correct, it might not have been entered in your diary. Let me put the question in another way. Whom did you see on the night of October 6th?"

Bigot felt that his interrogation was going with surprising ease. For some reason which could scarcely have had any innocent explanation, the little deputy was again reduced to a state of panic. Bigot took advantage of this to drop some of his customary suavity. There was no question now as to who was conducting the interrogation. Quesnay was ready to come and feed out of his hand.

"Yes, monsieur, I want an answer to that question. Whom did you see on the night of October 6th?"

"I may have seen a number of people; just as you yourself have to see people without thinking it worth while to note the fact in your diary."

"I am not talking of a number of people; I am asking you about one particular person whom you saw late that evening."

"Listen, monsieur; I do not know what rank you hold in the police; I do not even know your name. I presume that I have a right to ask."

"Certainly you have. I am Inspector Bigot of the ninth *arrondissement*."

"Well, M. Bigot, it is not necessary for me to tell you my name; you know it; but you may not know how I stand with my political party. Let me ask you this. Are you a freemason?"

"Well, no, monsieur, not yet, but I have often thought I should like to belong to the fraternity."

"Ah! Then you could have no better supporter in your candidature than myself. I say this without arrogance. I have worked hard for the brotherhood, and I am prepared to work harder still. You would find it very advantageous in your profession to be a freemason, quite apart from the satisfaction it would give you to be able to help some brother freemason who has fallen into the hands of the police through no fault of his own. But in this case I am more than a mere freemason. Hints have been dropped to me that I am approaching the critical stage in my career. A year hence, they say, I may be offered a very important portfolio, more so than that of Minister of Education, with the power to recompense my friends. You, for example, you have ambitions—don't deny it—everyone has ambitions—you have brains; you ought to rise rapidly in your profession—more rapidly than you have hitherto. Now, suppose that I were offered the portfolio of Minister of the Interior; the Ministry would be sure to send for the dossier of Inspector Bigot of the ninth *arrondissement* and ask why he has not been noted for early promotion..."

A wave of self-esteem seized upon Bigot in spite of his sense of duty. After all, thought he, surely this is not the kind of man that self-seeking politicians would entrust with so coveted a portfolio as that of Minister of the Interior. Still, with such a strange breed as politicians, one never knows. These thoughts ran through Bigot's head, while his face wore an enigmatic smile. Quesnay thought that this was a sign that he was prevailing.

"I am forgetting my duties as a host, monsieur. Please forgive me." He went to a little cupboard and took out a bottle and two glasses. "My friends tell me that this is an excellent Armagnac. I should like to have your opinion of it. It comes from a vineyard in my own country. Indeed, as a boy I was present when it was distilled."

Bigot waved it aside, but the deputy insisted. "You must at least do me the honour of tasting it." He filled the two glasses and carried one of them to Bigot. Both took a prolonged sip at the potent liquor. "As I was saying, by dear inspector, I am reaching the turning-point in my career. Happily, you civil servants know nothing of the anxieties of political men who have tried to do their duty by their constituents and by their country. There comes a moment to us all when the slightest breath of scandal, be it ever so ill-founded, may blow the most promising career to the winds. For example..."

Bigot waited eagerly for what was coming. "You were saying?"

"Exactly, my dear chief inspector—don't think I am anticipating, since very soon that will be your official title—we understand each other. No one, however upright he may be, can always escape the shafts of calumny. Jealousy, my friend, is the cardinal human sin; detraction is the common weapon of the envious. Granted, for the sake of argument, that I did see someone on that fatal night of October 6th, what of it? The thing is done every day. Cite me any of the great names in political circles during the past ten years and I will tell you strange stories about each of them. But what of it? All have lived them down, and many of them have had public funerals, and, let it be well understood, have bequeathed considerable sums to their heirs."

Their glasses were now three-quarters empty. Bigot's expression was solemn. Armagnac always had this effect upon him. "You must understand, my dear monsieur, that orders must be obeyed; that justice must be done."

"What do you mean?" asked Quesnay in a twitter of alarm.

"Let me say this. I do not believe that you were actually the guilty person, but I call upon you to give me the name of that person."

"Ah, no. You are asking something that no honourable man would divulge, and, thank God, I am an honourable man. No, *par example*; not the name."

At this critical moment an electric bell from the front door of the flat began to tinkle. Quesnay sprang to his feet. He appeared strangely agitated. "You will excuse me, my friend. This is a visitor from the Chamber who comes to me with an urgent message. It would not be becoming if he found you here. For once will you submit to a little ruse? I shall bring him into this room, and you will conceal yourself for one minute behind that curtain in the entrance hall, and as soon as I have taken him into this room and closed the door you will slip out. We will meet again to-morrow."

"At what time?"

"Well, let us say at the same hour as to-day." The bell rang again—this time persistently. "Quick, my dear friend, behind this curtain. Farewell until to-morrow."

Behind his curtain Bigot heard the front door open and the words, "Ah! My dear M. Tissot, this is indeed a pleasure." And a strange voice answered:

"I was not sure that it was prudent to call upon you here, monsieur, but I fear something has leaked out, and—"

"This way," said Quesnay's voice, urging his new guest into the sitting-room. The door was shut behind them.

Bigot lingered for a few moments in the hope of listening to the conversation, but the house was too well-built for that; not a sound came through the massive door. He let himself out to the staircase and was soon in the street.

His first act was to jot down the few words he had overheard from behind his curtain while they were still fresh in his memory.

He did this by the light from a shop window. What had begun to leak out? The fact that those two men had been concerned in a murder, or was it some other disreputable act in which they had both taken part? It was, at any rate, a good starting-point for the adjourned interrogation on the morrow.

Tissot, who was he? There was no time to waste; Bigot went straight to the post office in the rue Amsterdam and consulted the telephone directory. There were no less than twenty-three subscribers named Tissot; it would need a whole day to determine which of them was acquainted with the deputy Jules Quesnay, and this was work which could not be entrusted to any subordinate.

When he returned to his office in the rue de la Rochefoucault he called in the clerk and gave some hasty directions about visiting the various persons named Tissot, omitting those whom he had reserved for himself because they were all in his own *arrondissement*.

Surely the little god who broods over deserving detectives was watching over Bigot that next morning, since at the office of the second Tissot whom he had reserved for personal interrogation he struck what he believed to be a vein of the purest gold. The man had an office in a courtyard with four separate staircases: one given up to a cardboard-box-maker; a second to a dentist; a third to a truss manufacturer, and a fourth to a builder; this builder was M. Tissot, a thin, nervous-looking person with a reserve of forced *bonhomie* always on tap. Following the direction on the door, Bigot entered without knocking, and found the man he sought closeted with a lady of redundant figure who acted as his amanuensis. Bigot showed him his card, and M. Tissot hastened to intimate to his stout secretary that her presence was undesired. She cast a swift look at the visitor; one glance was enough for her—she fled like a frightened rabbit.

"M. Tissot? Good. Now that you are alone, allow me to ask you a question—a very simple one. Whom did you go to see after office hours on the night of Tuesday, October 6th?"

The confusion in Tissot's face was painful to behold; he changed from red to white and back again to red like a politician who changes his party. He came to a decision. "I remember the 6th of October very well. It was my brother's birthday. When I closed the office I went straight to his apartment and spent the evening there."

"Your brother's name and address?"

Tissot gave them readily, knowing that a call on the telephone would provide corroborative evidence, but Bigot had ringing in his ears the words, "I fear something has leaked out," and became convinced that the voice of the man now speaking to him was that of Quesnay's visitor of the evening before. He drew his bow at a venture. "I am referring to the gentleman you visited last night—the deputy whom you told that something had leaked out."

M. Tissot was struck speechless. He gasped with his mouth open like a newly landed fish, but after swallowing audibly once or twice he found his voice. "I refuse to answer. You have your own remedy, monsieur. Since you know so much already, go and question the man I saw. I did nothing except at his instigation. He is the man that counted. I see what's happened. He set a trap for me last night. He had hidden you away in that apartment of his in order that you might take a note of everything we said. Well, you can do your worst. When the time comes I shall have something to say, but you can't force me to speak now."

"You mean that it was you who committed the crime at his instigation?"

Tissot had turned mulish. "I refuse to speak. You must get it all out of him."

Bigot had achieved his object. He knew now that out of the twenty-three Tissots in the telephone directory this was his man. Throughout the day he had to decide between two courses: either to do his duty without fear or favour, or to give time for his patron in the unseen world to work a miracle on his behalf—to move Quesnay to procure his (Bigot's) promotion. To anyone outside political and police circles it might seem perilously near blackmail, but in both these callings in France the moral aspect of a transaction is the last to be considered if scandal be avoided. He had felt so sure that he was on the point of discovering the perpetrator of the crime that when Verneuil and his Englishman from Scotland Yard came to him during the morning to seek authority for arresting the foreign swindlers in connection with the murder, he laughed at them. Should he startle that stolid English detective by bringing in the murderer and his instigator, or should he quietly allow his own promotion to be worked for him?

The knotty point had not been unravelled when Bigot rang the bell at the Quesnay flat. The bell was answered not by Quesnay himself, but by a hungry-looking youth who described himself as M. Quesnay's secretary, and stated that the deputy was expected every moment from the Chamber; that he had left instructions that M. Bigot should be shown into the *salon* to await him.

It was a dreary little room to have to wait in. He strolled over to study the details of a bronze statuette on a marble base, representing a lady in classical dress with a discarded harp behind her, and an expression as who should say "I shall never learn to play this damned instrument." It was an epitome of the art of the third empire.

A latch-key grated in the door. Jules Quesnay bustled in. The sepulchral voice of the "secretary" gave an affirmative answer to his question whether anyone was waiting to see him, and Bigot became convinced that the "secretary" had been brought there to qualify as a witness, to deny, if necessary, everything that passed at the interview. He would be listening at the key-hole in all probability; it would not be needful for him to overhear the conversation, in fact he would have a freer hand to describe it if he had not overheard a word.

Quesnay was almost boisterous in his welcome. "Ah, my friend, you have taken me at the foot of the letter. You've had time to think things over."

"Not only to think things over, *monsieur le Ministre*, but to question the man you saw on October 6th and again last night."

"I thought that we were going to deal with this matter quietly as between friends; there was no need for you to see M. Tissot. I hinted to you, and I can put the matter more firmly than in a hint, that it would be to your advantage to take no further notice of this affair."

"That is all very well, but in a serious matter like this—I've got the British Embassy to consider."

"The British Embassy?" Quesnay stared at him in blank astonishment. "The British Embassy has nothing whatever to do with the building of a school for zoology for children at Vincennes."

It was now Bigot's turn to register astonishment.

Quesnay was the first to find the key to this comedy of errors. "Do you seriously mean to say that you thought I had a hand in the murder of that young man? It is time for us to lay our cards on the table. It is perfectly true that I did offer to M. Tissot to use my influence to get him the job of building the school; that I did tell him that one good turn deserves another; that he did promise me a certain commission, and if you like to make it public I did touch that commission before the contract was signed; but if you do make it public, I shall reserve to myself the right of pointing out that when criminal investigation is entrusted to men like the inspector of the ninth *arrondissement*, it is not surprising that crimes go unpunished."

"I understand, monsieur, we are in a sense opposed to one another, but, in another sense, we may call ourselves allies."

Quesnay rose and went to the cupboard for the bottle and glasses. "Let us cement the alliance," he said.

Chapter Nineteen

DETECTIVE SERGEANT COOPER had relieved his boredom by visiting the sights of Paris. He was full of enthusiasm for Napoleon's resting-place at the Invalides.

"To think that that little blighter from Corsica damned nearly conquered all Europe, and would have invaded England if Nelson and Wellington hadn't been there to stop him."

Richardson tapped his foot impatiently.

"Oh, I forgot, you've seen it all before, but I tell you, inspector, that the sight of that little tomb in the basement set me thinking."

"I have the present to think of, not the past. Have you seen anything of that little gang with the gold brick?"

"Not a word. I suppose they'll turn up on Monday for my final answer."

Richardson began to pace the room. "It's no good pretending that we're getting on. We have struck a bad patch, and if we don't mind our step there will be a row with the Foreign Office about our expenses."

"I don't suppose you've been idle these last two days."

"No, I've been to the Zoo with Verneuil, and we've established the fact that a platinum blonde woman took one of those photographs from the back of the wolves' cages. If she was

Pinet's woman, then either she or Pinet let the film drop in the murdered man's room."

"Well, that's something surely. Pinet admitted that he had visited the flat on the night of the murder. Why should he have denied that he or his wife had a camera of just that size? If he was innocent he would have told the whole truth. It's no crime to photograph animals at the Zoo. Wouldn't Verneuil consent to search that villa from top to bottom?"

"He would. In fact, he told me that he intended to, but if we find the camera and interrogate those two people to within an inch of their lives, we shan't have enough evidence to convict the murderer. No, I'm not going to trust to Verneuil. I'm going down this very evening to le Pecq to do a spell of quiet observation on that villa. You can't come with me in that kit; they'd spot you a mile off."

"But look here, inspector, you mustn't leave me without final orders as to what I'm to say to these gold-brick blighters when I see them to-morrow."

"I shall be back to-night. There will be plenty of time to decide that point to-morrow morning."

The rush hour was just beginning when Richardson took his return ticket to le Pecq; the platform and the carriage were crowded with season ticket-holders, many of them going through to St. Germain. A train was about to leave, but since every seat in the second class was occupied, Richardson became a strap-hanger. At Croissy passengers poured out of the train; the number going through to le Pecq and St. Germain was not large. Indeed, when the train pulled up at that station, Richardson was the only second-class passenger to alight; only one man got down from the first-class coach and ran down into the subway before Richardson reached the steps. The platform lights were dim, but there was something familiar about the walk, and when the figure was between him and the station-lamp at the exit, recognition came in a flash; it was Pinet himself. For a moment Richardson decreased the distance between them with some vague instinct to keep the other man in view, but quite suddenly he caught sight of a lady, waiting under the lamp outside the station, and its rays glinted on hair the colour of bronzed silver. He was perhaps seven yards behind Pinet when the two met, and he heard the woman demand, without any greeting, "Have you brought the evening papers?" and the man's reply, "Yes, three of them, but there's not a word about her."

"Perhaps they didn't think a woman of the *pave* worth while." The man grunted and Richardson heard no more.

It being unsafe to follow the pair too closely, Richardson gave them a start of two or three minutes; they were quickly lost to view in the ill-lighted avenue which led to their villa; when Richardson came abreast of the villa, the shutters were closed and not a glimmer of light could be seen. He looked for a convenient observation post and found one in the muddy little lane which ran at right-angles to the tarred highway on which the villa looked out. It was a fairly substantial pine tree within five yards of the lane; anyone standing behind it to watch the house would be entirely invisible from the windows. Opposite to this post stood the garage.

Richardson found one strong drawback to his observation post; the place was infested with mosquitoes of the predatory and hungry species with striped legs; they attacked his face, neck and hands, and when he attempted to defend himself they made his socks and ankles their point of attack, even crawling up his trouser leg and plunging their weapons into his bare skin. A police officer on observation duty cannot spend his time slapping himself without asking for trouble; the pest had to be borne in spartan silence.

How long the torture was to be endured became the question of the moment. Probably these people were sitting snugly round their supper-table, scanning the columns of the evening papers, and here was he, marooned in a mosquito swamp without any hope of returning to Paris with a discovery to the good. The futility of this self-imposed task of observation filled his mind, when suddenly a shaft of light shot across the main road on his left; the front door had been opened. It was closed a second or two later, leaving a darkness that could be felt. But there were sounds—heel-taps on the tarred road; the heels of two persons who could not keep step. They were approaching him down the muddy lane; they stopped at the garage and unlocked it, as could be heard by the grating of the key.

"Stand there," said a man's voice. "I will run the car out."

The garage doors were swung back; the door of the car was opened and shut; the headlights were switched on. They would have risked disclosing Richardson had they been in their normal position, but they were dipping headlights and they were dipped. The self-starter whirred; the engine roared; the car began to move.

The headlights shone upon the second person waiting in the road; it was, as Richardson suspected, the woman they knew as the "platinum blonde." Her feet were in a pool of light; she was wearing black shoes, but these were secured by fancy laces of black and white plaid. Where had he seen laces like these before? Suddenly the recollection came to him. The wad of notes which the sick woman had under her pillow had been tied with a shoe-lace of exactly this pattern.

The two people exchanged places after talking for two or three minutes in low tones. The woman took the wheel, waved a gloved hand to Pinet, and slipped in her clutch. The car turned in the direction of Paris and gathered speed. Richardson could not move from his observation post until the man was safely within doors. He did some quick thinking. Somehow he must discover the streamline car, painted scarlet and beige, in Paris, for to Paris it was obvious that its driver was going. He could not follow her; if he were to charter a car from the garage opposite the station and order the driver to overtake Pinet's car, the news would certainly filter through to Pinet that a foreigner, speaking French with an accent, was on his track. This was not to be thought of. There was one other way—to take the next train to St. Lazare; to taxi to the Place Vendôme, where the woman had parked her car on the last occasion, and trust to luck that she had done this a second time. And here was Pinet fooling about in the garage with the light turned on when every minute counted.

At last that cursed light was switched off, the garage doors clanged to and locked and a shadowy figure, more imagined than seen, was on its way to the front gate. He must still wait until he saw a light from the front door. Ah! There it was! Bang went the door and Richardson was alone with the mosquitoes. He covered the distance in record time; a train clattered in; it was nearly empty; he found a seat in a second class and wondered whether the train would be run as an express from Croissy to St. Lazare. It was, for this was used as a theatre train by the good people of the suburbs.

At this hour the traffic in Paris was thinning. Richardson jumped into a taxi and directed the driver to drop him at the corner of the rue de la Paix and the Place Vendôme, and paid him off with a liberal *pourboire* for the speed he had used. The Paris taxi-driver is seldom interested in the business of his fares; otherwise this one might have wondered why a passenger who had urged him to speed should have sauntered off among the parked cars as if he had the entire night before him. But he swung round and drove off in the direction of the station. The Place Vendôme was fairly crowded with parked cars ranged in lines, and others were joining the ranks every moment. The lighting was not good enough to show up even the most gaudily painted car; one had to pass along the ranks to find the car one wanted. Richardson drew blank in those on the right side of the square, the woman's usual parking-place, and had just begun a scrutiny of the cars on the other side when he caught sight of a gaudy scarlet and beige car just in front of him. Yes, it was the car he was looking for, he knew the number; but through the back window he could see a woman's hat. The car was occupied and he must not risk being seen and recognized. Who was she waiting for? Not the man she was living with; she had left him behind at le Pecq. He ran rapidly over in his mind the little discovery he had made of the shoe-laces which matched that he had seen round the bundle of notes. Was this one of the lucky coincidences which so often step in to help the fortunate detective?

Was this woman in the car in a position to pay over to a woman of the *trottoir* a sum of several thousand francs? It must be blackmail; there could be no other explanation. But again— where did the money come from? Dimly within his mind an idea began to take shape. Perhaps the platinum blonde had some hold over another person—a successful politician for example— and it was he who had provided the money to be paid to the blackmailer. So he was quite prepared to see a man approach the scarlet and beige car, and he determined to change his place for another which commanded a nearer view of the car. His plan was quickly made. He would follow the man until he discovered his address.

And then, as so often happens in police work, it was the unexpected that supervened. He was standing quite close to a shabby, old-fashioned car with rusty, battered wings and all the other marks of a car bought second-hand, when a woman came quietly past him, walking down the ranks of the car park. She gave him a quick look, probably mistaking him for the owner of the antediluvian vehicle by which he was standing. The light was poor, but there was something familiar to him about her profile. He could not have sworn to her identity in any court;

it was only a vague impression that linked her with the sick woman he had seen in bed that morning—the woman who kept her money tied up with a variegated shoe-lace. Her dress and walk had the cheap, flashy aspect of her profession; a whiff of cheap perfume assailed his nostrils as she passed. It required no great gift of intuition to guess that this was the person awaited by the platinum blonde. He had only to wait to see the meeting to know what his next move was to be.

A moment later the woman caught sight of the car she was looking for and went straight to it through the intervening ranks. Richardson saw the two women in conversation and wormed his way through the lines of cars until he had a view of them through the windows of the vehicle nearest to the platinum blonde's. To judge from the gestures of the two it was not a friendly meeting. At one point both voices were raised, but he was not near enough to hear what they were saying. The point was that they had lost sight of the possibility of eavesdroppers. One sentence he did catch and understand; it came from the lips of the platinum blonde in the strident tone adopted by Frenchwomen when they are incensed.

"I tell you that I haven't another *sou* to give you —not a *sou*."

And then the other woman said something which blunted the edge of the discussion, for the voices lost some of their acerbity. Pinet's lady extruded a long, silk-covered leg from the car, following it with the rest of her person—wound up the windows, locked up the car, and led the way towards the pavement. Richardson took a more devious course to the other side of the rue de la Paix and kept them well in view. They crossed the road and made for the Café de la Paix in the Boulevard; he did the same.

He was not the kind of man to take risks when he was, as he thought, nearing his goal. Both these women had seen him at different times dressed in the same clothes that he was then wearing—obviously clothes of English cut. Both of them were engaged in transactions that would not bear the light of day. Fortunately there was more than one door into the Café de la Paix. They had gone in through that on the Boulevard; he chose the one leading from the Place de l'Opera. The café was crowded; the two women found seats near the entrance and were too busy in conversation to notice him; he made for the only vacant seat, which was actually next to their table, and turned his back on them.

After having given their order Thérèse left her seat for a few minutes; the waiter returned with the beverage and filled the glasses; then Thérèse returned and said laughingly, "You won't mind, my dear, if we exchange glasses; it is more prudent."

The platinum blonde broke into a hard laugh. "I know that you don't mean what you say, that it's a jest to make me smile, because of course you could not really believe the story you told me just now. These doctors, my dear… they know nothing. I could tell you a story of a friend of mine…" She had dropped her voice and Richardson never learned the dramatic fate of the friend of hers.

He did not strain his ears to listen to the rest of their conversation, for he had now plenty to occupy his thoughts. It was obvious from what he had just heard that Thérèse had not told Verneuil the whole story; that she had either intentionally or through inadvertence concealed the fact that she had had a drink with this same companion on the evening when she was taken ill, and that she had guessed, rightly or wrongly, that her liquor had been doped; otherwise why should she have insisted on changing glasses with her hostess? That the platinum blonde was her hostess was quickly established. She had tinkled her glass for the bill, paid it and was now taking leave of Thérèse.

"Until Monday," were her parting words.

As soon as she was out of sight Thérèse summoned the waiter and asked for a glass of cognac. Richardson had decided to keep observation on her rather than follow the other woman back to le Pecq, but scarcely had the waiter brought the cognac when a new figure entered the café—no less a person than Polowski. Fortunately Richardson had a newspaper before his face at the moment when Polowski was making a survey of the assemblage. He was about to take a vacant seat when the woman Thérèse jumped up and went across to him. He was politeness itself— hat off, back curved, deferential bow. She invited him to her table, but he declined no less politely on the excuse that he was awaiting guests, and a little crestfallen she returned to her seat to sip her cognac.

Suddenly the scheme of things was disclosed to Richardson's mind. Luck had favoured him that evening. The platinum blonde was paying blackmail to this waif Thérèse; the platinum blonde had been visited by Polowski and his little gang. Polowski was acquainted with Thérèse. Whatever might be the connection between these three persons, it was clear that the explanation must be sought for at the villa in le Pecq. It was needless now to follow Thérèse; he would go and take counsel with his subordinate, who was known to the staff of the Grand Hotel as the eccentric French Canadian, M. Rivaux.

Chapter Twenty

"M. Rivaux is alone," announced the resplendent porter of the Grand Hotel.

"He's had visitors this evening?"

"No, monsieur, no visitors."

"You need not announce me; he is expecting me," said Richardson, going towards the lift.

He knocked at the door of Cooper's room and was admitted immediately.

"Let us sit down," said Richardson. "I've been having a lively time. Let me tell you exactly what's happened since I saw you after tea."

He proceeded to describe his adventures at le Pecq and afterwards in the Place Vendôme. Cooper listened to him with close attention.

"The plot is thickening," he said; "but where do I come in?"

"You have a very important part to play. Here are all these people—the three swindlers with the gold brick; Pinet and his platinum blonde woman; that street-walker, who apparently was given a dose of something that disagreed with her, and who is receiving considerable sums of money from Pinet's woman. How do all these people come to know one another? What is the link between them? That is where you come in, Cooper. You have to find the answer to the conundrum."

"The devil I have!

"Instead of waiting for these men to call upon you on Monday, you must telephone to them and make an appointment for to-morrow, Sunday. They will think that everything is going swimmingly, especially if you say that you've had a cable from your bank in Quebec. When they do come, you must take a high and mighty line with them—say that you don't care to play second fiddle to a French adventurer; that you thought they were dealing with you alone, and now you find that they are in treaty with another man behind your back."

"If I tell them that, they'll want to know who my informant was."

"Well, the answer to that is quite simple. Your informant was a woman whom you picked up in the street and took to a café, and she was half seas over at the time—*in vino veritas*, as they used to say at school. That was her stage of intoxication when she blurted out the story of an adventure she had had. You need not fill in any details. You must use your own discretion, but you must get out of them their reason for going to Pinet's villa in le Pecq."

"I'm supposed to give them a final answer about that gold from Russia."

"Well, then, you've got a good excuse for putting off any final answer—that you want a full explanation as to the business that took them to Pinet's house in le Pecq. When you get the explanation out of them you must stipulate for another two days before giving your answer. If they haven't been taken in by our friend Verneuil before Monday and they come round to see M. Rivaux at this hotel, they'll find that the gentleman has left for Canada without giving an address. But from what I know of Verneuil, I fancy that they will all be safely under lock and key by Monday."

"Can I leave this hotel to-morrow night? I shan't be sorry, I can tell you."

"Yes. As soon as you've bowed your friends out, you'll take a taxi round to Mr. Gregory's flat. I'll warn him to expect you. There you will take off your fancy dress and come round to our hotel clothed and in your right mind. I'll ask Mr. Gregory to come round to this hotel to collect your baggage, and tell them that you've been summoned home by cable. How does that strike you?"

"It strikes me that since I saw you a few hours ago you seem pretty sure that you're on the right tack; that we're going to clear the business up."

"There's many a slip, my friend; it's better not to feel sure until success falls into your lap."

"I'm entitled to my own view, inspector. Whenever I've known you with that confident look in your eye, everything is coming out right."

"Never mind what you notice in my eye, because I want to shut both of them for the next eight hours. Good night."

Before ten o'clock next morning Richardson presented himself at the headquarters of the ninth *arrondissement* and asked for M. Verneuil.

"I have some news for you, M. Verneuil," he announced.

"Perhaps I've something for *you*, monsieur," replied Verneuil, screwing up his eyes. "We shall find M. Bigot ready to feed out of our hands this morning."

"Indeed? What has happened?"

"Ah! That one can only guess at. He had an interview yesterday with M. Quesnay. What passed at that interview is known only to M. Quesnay, M. Bigot, and the all-seeing eye above us—but Bigot has now changed his tune a little. What have you to report?"

"I went down to le Pecq last night and I made a little discovery. You remember how that bundle of notes we saw in that sick woman's room was tied up?"

"Perfectly; with a new-fangled black and white shoe-lace that a few women are wearing now."

"Exactly. That woman of Pinet's at le Pecq was wearing the same kind of shoe-lace last night."

"Very possibly. It's the kind of novelty that captivates women of that class."

"That's not all. I followed the lady up to Paris; she parked her car in the Place Vendôme, and the woman Thérèse, whom we had seen in the morning, came to meet her there."

Verneuil's eyes narrowed to mere slits. "So they know one another, those two?"

"Yes, and they went off together to the Café de la Paix and had a drink together."

"Very possible, that. It doesn't surprise me."

"And while Thérèse was away a moment from their table the waiter brought their drinks. When she returned she insisted on exchanging glasses with Pinet's woman."

"She did?"

"Yes, and Pinet's woman tried to laugh it off."

"You haven't wasted your time, monsieur," said Verneuil. "You may not be actually on the track of that murderer you're in search of, but you have brought me something to look into. I shall have to see that woman Thérèse again."

"Stop, I haven't finished. You don't know, perhaps, that the woman Thérèse is acquainted with those swindlers with the gold brick."

"How do you know that, monsieur?"

"By pure luck. While I was in the Café de la Paix watching the woman, in walked Polowski; she went over to his table and greeted him."

"She may have had an eye to business."

Richardson shook his head. "No; he was an old friend of hers, I could see."

Verneuil scrutinized Richardson with an appraising eye. "You may not be so far from a solution of the murder mystery as we thought, monsieur. M. Bigot is in his room at this moment. He expressed a wish to see you when you called at the station again. I suggest that we go and see him now."

It was quite a different Bigot who received them in his room—a chastened Bigot who had little to say about the work that had occupied him. "I regret, monsieur, that some very pressing work which called for tact these last few days prevented me from giving full attention to the work you are doing. Now that I am more at liberty I suggest that we sit down and go over together everything that you have discovered so far."

For an hour and a quarter they discussed what the reader has already heard. Bigot, dismounted from his high horse, proved to be quite intelligent and ready to entertain suggestions from his colleagues of the Metropolitan Police in London; indeed, he was a thought over-ready to take decisive action in respect of Richardson's friends with the gold brick. Richardson tried to restrain him by pointing out that the most useful act for the moment would be to get the truth out of the woman Thérèse.

"H'm," remarked Bigot dubiously. "To get the truth out of a woman like that..."

Richardson stooped to flattery. "I am sure, monsieur, that if you undertake the interrogation, even of a woman like that, you will make her talk."

"I think that if I have her down here to interrogate, we shall get more out of her than we should if we went to see her in her own lodgings. M. Verneuil, let it be your task to bring her down here. As for the men with the gold brick, what is your opinion, M. Richardson?"

"I should like to let my colleague have his interview with them before they are detained by the police, because my colleague may elicit good grounds for arresting them. To-morrow, in any case, they might be detained for interrogation."

"Very well, let it be as you say, monsieur. A ring on the telephone from you will suffice to bring about their detention."

"Very good, monsieur. I have some business to attend to at the British Embassy, so I will leave you, but if you will allow me I propose to come round later in the day—say at six o'clock—to hear what that woman has had to say."

"I hope you will tell the Embassy that we police of the ninth *arrondissement* are doing all that we can to help you."

"Certainly, monsieur; I shall not fail to convey that information," said Richardson, taking his leave.

On his arrival at the gate of the British Embassy, Richardson received a shock. The uniformed porter at the gate lifted his eyebrows in astonishment at the request to see Mr. Gregory.

"I'm sorry, sir, but Mr. Gregory does not come here on Sundays unless he's taking his turn for duty."

"Sunday!" exclaimed Richardson. "I've been so busy that I had quite forgotten that it was Sunday."

"That is nothing to be surprised at, sir. Here in Paris they carry on exactly as if it was a weekday all the morning, but I fancy that you'll find Mr. Gregory at his flat until lunch-time. Would you like me to telephone to him that you're coming?"

"I wish you would."

The porter retired to his lodge and engaged in conversation with an unseen speaker. He came out nodding his head. "You'll find Mr. Gregory at home and expecting you," he said.

A taxi conveyed Richardson to the flat. On Sundays, he gathered, the third secretary was not an early riser. He found him still in dressing-gown and slippers.

"Sit down, inspector, and tell us what you've been doing for us and what we can do for you."

"You've done so much for me, sir," replied Richardson, "that I scarcely like to ask for more, but the important point is that I think we are getting on, and that I can now safely recall my colleague, Sergeant Cooper, from posing as a Canadian capitalist."

Gregory laughed. "Your colleague must be a loss to the British stage," he said. "Did no one find him out?"

"No, sir; at the hotel everyone thinks that he is the genuine article, but his work is now done. The French police intend to detain those Polish rascals who pretend to be selling gold as soon as they have had their last interview with M. Rivaux, the Canadian, who will be called back to Canada by cable, and will quietly drop his disguise at your flat and reappear at my hotel as Sergeant Cooper. It would be a great service if you would send round to the Grand Hotel for his luggage and settle his bill (of course at my expense), at the same time telling them that he has been cabled for to Canada."

"I shall do it myself, inspector, but it is fair to warn you that I shall expect your chiefs at the Yard to recommend me for the C.B."

"You deserve far more than the C.B., sir, for what you've done for us," said Richardson, who was not deceived by his serious tone, and was equally solemn in his reply.

"What time do you think that your Mr. Cooper—my M. Rivaux—will come round to my flat, deflated like a punctured tyre? Because I ought to be there."

"I believe he was to see the men just after lunch-time, say at two o'clock."

"And if he comes out alive he ought to be round at my flat by about three. You know, inspector, I'm running a most frightful risk. Suppose they follow him to my flat and he disappears; they may denounce me to the police, and the papers will come out with double headlines, 'Murder of a Canadian Millionaire by a British Diplomat. Concealment of the Body.'"

Richardson's face betrayed quiet amusement. "I don't think they'll follow him, sir, because I have arranged with the police of the ninth *arrondissement* that they shall wait in the street outside and take Cooper's friends into custody."

"On what charge?"

"On suspicion to start with, sir—suspicion of murder, if you like—and then, if that charge cannot be sustained, they will be quietly expelled from the country and the gate put up behind them. So you see they won't know anything about Cooper's subsequent movements."

"You sleuths from the Yard are wonderful people. You seem to think of everything."

"I wish we did, sir."

"Luckily, inspector, this is Sunday. I can give up my game of golf and be at home all the afternoon. Where are you going now, if it's not an improper question?"

"Not at all, sir. I'm going to get some lunch."

"'*Les beaux esprits se rencontrent,*' as they say over here. I suppose that when you're hungry you walk into the first place that looks like a restaurant. Now to-day you have the chance of a lifetime. With me as your guide you shall taste real French cooking at its best. Come along, this is my show."

Gregory maintained his reputation as an epicurean at that midday feast. It will not be fair to say here where he took his guest, but it was a little place where the owner was pleased to give friendly hints to his guests, and where the wife charged herself with the cooking.

The proprietor had been, so Gregory said, *maître d'hôtel* to Cardinal Rampolla. They lunched well. Gregory feasted also upon the stories of his guest, which he elicited with all the cunning accredited to diplomatists. His only complaint was that his guest was too abstemious in the matter of vintage.

They walked together to Gregory's flat and sat waiting for Cooper. At last the bell rang. Gregory ran to answer it. Richardson heard him say, "At last, M. Rivaux. You will find an old acquaintance of yours waiting for you."

Cooper's make-up was beginning to show signs of wear in a strong light, but he was buoyed up by the thought that in a few minutes he was to be freed from his disguise for ever. It was a vain thought. The inexorable Richardson was lying in wait for him in the sitting-room and there was no escape.

"Now, Cooper, let me hear the worst. Did the men come?"

"Yes, they came all right."

"Did they tell you why they went down to le Pecq to see that fellow Pinet?"

"Yes; they'd heard that he was a millionaire, and they hoped to stick him with their gold brick, but he wasn't having any. Of course, when they told the story to me the gold brick was genuine bullion."

"A millionaire? Was he playing the same part as you?"

"No; according to them he had won five million francs in the French State lottery."

"I was always under the impression," interrupted Gregory, "that no one ever won a *sou* in the State lottery except the State."

Richardson took no notice of this flippant interjection. "And Pinet wouldn't bite?"

"No; they showed him the gold brick and scraped off a little genuine gold dust for him to get tested by experts, but he wouldn't be drawn."

"Ah!" said Richardson, "that explains that scarlet and beige car in which his woman drives about, but it doesn't make it clear why Pinet should be paying hush-money to that wretched woman who had eaten something that disagreed with her."

"What woman?" asked Gregory eagerly. "You seem to have been keeping queer company, inspector."

"Yes, sir, I have. I happened to be with a detective of the ninth *arrondissement* when he was called in by a *concierge* to question a woman who was believed to have been poisoned. It's a longish story, which I'll tell you another time. At this moment Sergeant Cooper is badly in need of a wash and brush-up. When he is re-converted into a Christian we'll get him to tell us exactly how his interview with the gold brick gentlemen went. By the way, Cooper, you may be relieved to know that those gentry were taken in by the French police as they were leaving the hotel this afternoon."

"On what charge?" asked Cooper.

"I don't suppose that any charge has been formulated yet. The French police have wider powers than ours in London. If they don't like the look of you they take you in and make you give an account of yourself from the day when you were born, and while you're being put through it they go down and search your lodging."

Chapter Twenty-One

WHILE COOPER was locked in the bathroom, Richardson related to his host how he had discovered the association of Thérèse Volny with Pinet's housekeeper, the woman with the beige and scarlet car.

"At this moment Thérèse ought to be at the police station, undergoing what corresponds to the 'third degree' in America, and we have promised to go down this evening and hear the result."

"Lord! To think that this kind of thing is going on under one's nose, while one is leading a sheltered life in the Chancery of the British Embassy. You have given me a new respect for Paris as the city of adventure. I'd always heard stories of what Scotland Yard can do when it wakes up and begins to take notice, and they are now confirmed in every particular." Gregory cocked his ear. "I think I hear our late Canadian millionaire stirring. Be prepared for an agreeable shock. Here he comes."

Certainly it was a shock. Richardson scrutinized his colleague with a critical eye and had to admit to himself that the disguise had been complete, for here was the detective sergeant that he knew, and M. Rivaux from the French colony in Quebec had been left lying on the floor of Mr. Gregory's bathroom. Gregory cleared a chair for him.

"You'd better give us an account of your interview with those two men in your own way," said Richardson.

"There's not very much to tell. They came into my room looking pretty confident. They'd left their gold brick behind. I tackled them at once; said that it had come to my knowledge that they'd been dealing with another chap—a French journalist who lived at le Pecq. I took the high and mighty line. Who did they think they were dealing with when they came to me? I wasn't going to play second fiddle to any man. No, the deal was off. I told them that I had reason to believe that this was not the only journalist they had called upon. You see, inspector, I thought that I might jog them into coughing up an admission that they'd been to see Mr. Everett."

"Yes, that wasn't a bad move. Did it work?"

"I saw a look of blank surprise in both their faces and I came to the conclusion that Pinet was the only journalist they had approached. Then I tried to corner them. I asked them who had told them that Pinet had won the lottery, saying that I didn't believe a word of it; they'd gone to Pinet for quite another reason."

"I suppose they saw the names of the winners in some newspaper," said Richardson.

"Oh, no, inspector," observed Gregory. "They don't publish the names of the winners in this country—only the numbers of the winning tickets. Occasionally some weakling lets his friends know that he's won something and his name and address get into the papers. There was one poor devil—a miller he was—who had the whole pack at his heels trying to sell him things he didn't want. They actually made him buy a chateau that someone wanted to unload. But go on with your story, sergeant."

"I tried my hardest to get them to say how they had heard that Pinet had the winning ticket, but they stuck out that they couldn't remember who told them, but that it was common knowledge all over Paris. But I held to it, telling them that they'd have no difficulty in finding a purchaser for their gold, but that they could rule me out; I wouldn't touch their gold even if they brought it to me on a tray. You see, I was trying to bluff them into telling me a lot more about Pinet, but there was nothing doing. I don't believe that they knew anything about him except that he'd won the lottery, so that in that respect my play-acting was a wash-out."

"But surely they tried to soften you?"

"They did, and in the end I said that I would think it over between this afternoon and Monday, but they'll be in a place on Monday where they can't make calls on unsuspecting millionaires. By that time the police will have their gold brick to play with."

"You did very well, Cooper."

Cooper shook his head. "You might have said that, inspector, if I'd got out of them an admission that they'd called on Mr. Everett that night."

"One thing at a time; we are getting on, I think. And now we ought to be getting down to the police station to hear what the woman Thérèse has had to say." He rose from his chair to shake hands with Gregory. "I can't thank you enough, sir, for all you've done for us. I may have important news for you to-morrow morning—real 'stop-press' news."

Their arrival at the police station brought their first check. Verneuil, they were told, was out, but they could see M. Bigot if they wished. They did wish, and they found the man who was working his promotion enthroned on his office chair before an empty table.

"Ah, messieurs, I am very pleased to see you. You are no doubt anxious to hear what I have to report. My subordinate, Brigadier Verneuil, has been three times in search of the woman Thérèse, and has always been disappointed. The *concierge* was confident that she would be in this afternoon, and therefore I have sent him to the house a fourth time. If you will be patient he will soon be back, either with or without the woman. What have you been doing since I saw you last?"

"Sergeant Cooper has been interviewing those two men with the gold brick. You intended, I think, to detain them."

"Ah, yes. We have them here. We always find it best to let them cool their heels and the inside of their stomachs before putting them through the hoop."

"We will not detain you, monsieur," said Richardson, turning a blind eye to the empty writing-table. "We will wait in the room you were good enough to assign to us until M. Verneuil returns."

Bigot made no objection to the suggestion. He had found himself ill at ease in the presence of his English colleagues, whom he half suspected of guessing that he was using the case as a step to promotion while they were putting in solid work to solve it.

"As you will, messieurs. If the woman is found I will have her brought into your room for her examination; it is larger than this."

The two British detectives did not have long to wait. They had left the door ajar; quick steps sounded on the paved floor of the entrance; a woman's voice was raised in protest. Cooper went on tiptoe to the door, and returned to his seat. "It's Verneuil with a woman," he said.

Affairs do not run on oiled wheels in the Paris police stations. No one but the telephone operator in the head station of the ninth *arrondissement* seemed to have any fixed duties; they sat about awaiting orders. It was the telephone which kept them employed; when it reported a crime from some street in the *arrondissement,* a senior officer poked his head into the room where his subordinates were assembled and beckoned to the senior constable, who in turn selected a junior to accompany him. When they returned from their mission they spent time in writing out a voluminous report.

The woman who accompanied Verneuil was given a chair in the police waiting-room. She was quite at her ease; it was not the first time in her life that she had had to deal with policemen.

The first person to break in upon Richardson and Cooper was M. Bigot in person. "The woman is here, messieurs. I propose to examine her in this room, if you will kindly bring your chairs up to the head of the table. My place will be here." (He indicated the head of the table.) "The woman will sit in that chair at the bottom. If at any time during my examination a question occurs to you, I will ask you to write it down and pass it to me."

He stamped twice on the floor. Apparently it was a signal concerted with Verneuil, for a moment later that officer made his appearance, holding the woman Thérèse by the arm. Seeing that she had an audience she began to whimper.

"You are hurting my arm, monsieur. How can you treat a woman so? I shall have black bruises where your dirty fingers have pinched me."

The spectacle of the men seated at the head of the table seemed to sober her. Her eyes dwelt specially on Richardson, whom she seemed to recognize as someone whom she knew.

"I ask pardon, messieurs, but truly this police gentleman was hurting me."

"Sit down," commanded Bigot from the head of the table. He liked to show these British confreres how interrogations ought to be conducted. There was a mixture of brutal insistence and low cunning in his manner. "Your name is Thérèse Volny, I think," he began. "You live at 109 rue Vidal."

"Yes, sir." Her air of bravado had died out of her.

"How shall I describe your occupation? As a lady of leisure?"

"You can describe it in any way you think fit, monsieur."

"You carry a card, I suppose?"

"That goes without saying, monsieur. I am one who complies with the law."

"You have friends among the Paris journalists, I think."

"*Tenez!* Friends who are journalists! I do not stop to ask gentlemen what their occupation is. I take them as I find them."

"Come, come. You are perfectly aware of the occupation of one of your friends—a M. Pinet."

She furrowed her brow and shook her head. "I've never heard that name, monsieur."

Bigot assumed his most magisterial tone.

"I am asking you to confirm what we already know—that you are well acquainted with a gentleman who lives at le Pecq in the Seine-et-Oise."

She shook her head. "I can only repeat, monsieur, that I am acquainted with no such gentleman."

"You mean that I must bring M. Pinet into this room before you will admit that you know him? At that rate we may have to continue examining you until after midnight. Come, you have more sense than that?"

"Are you alluding to a gentleman who associates with a lady with blonde hair—blonde, I should say, from a few inches about the roots—black, or turning grey, nearer the scalp. Is that the gentleman you mean, monsieur? I am glad to learn from you that he is called Pinet."

"You knew perfectly well what his name was. And now you will have to tell me under what circumstances you first met him."

The woman screwed up her features. "How I first met him? We are then embarked upon ancient history. How does one meet a gentleman? When one asks him the time? When one finds him sitting all lonely in a café? Upon my word, I can't remember; it was so long ago."

"In any case you know him, madame, and you also know the lady he is now living with—the lady with blonde hair."

"Ah! That one! Who should not know her? At the cafés in Montmartre everyone knows Marthe Lacour. But if you ask me whether she is worth knowing I might reply in terms unfit for polite ears."

"You do not seem to like her? When you ask her for more money she is close-fisted?"

"What will you? The woman has millions, but would rather buy a new car than pay me what she owes me. How could she have touched a *sou* of this great fortune but for me?"

"And so she tries to stifle your lawful requests for more money by putting something in your drink?"

The woman fired up. "If I was sure that she had done that I'd—"

"Well," said Bigot, interrupting her, "you remember what happened the night before last. A woman doesn't suffer as you did unless someone had tampered with her liquor. And she had a motive, hadn't she? You had forced her to give you more money—you remember—the money that was tied up with a black and white shoe-lace. Now, if you want to be even with her, you have only to tell me the whole truth about what you did for M. Pinet."

"I have nothing to reproach M. Pinet with. It has been that woman all the time. I've done with her. What do you want to know, monsieur?"

"I want to know this. We are aware, of course, that this money that is being paid to you is hush-money. What service did you render to M. Pinet to give you a claim upon him?"

"Wouldn't you feel that you had a claim on a man if you'd brought him five millions? That's what I did for M. Pinet, monsieur, and then they dole me out a beggarly few thousands."

"But how did you bring him five millions?"

"By taking his lottery ticket to the Pavilion Flore and drawing out the money. How else?"

"Why didn't he go and draw it out himself?"

"Listen, monsieur. M. Pinet is an old friend of mine, though I hadn't seen him for months. A few days ago he came to look me up again and told me that he had the winning ticket for the National Lottery, but that he didn't dare to present it for fear that the other journalists would get to know of it and that every company promoter and beggar would be on his track. Would I take his ticket and claim the money? He would make it well worth my while if I would."

"And you did?"

"I did, monsieur. He followed me to the Pavilion and watched me draw the money. He waited for me outside. I paid it over to him and he put ten thousand francs into my hand, telling me not to speak to any journalist. Naturally I wasn't going to be satisfied with a beggarly ten thousand. I told him so and he was inclined to be more generous, but he let that woman come to the rendezvous instead of coming himself."

"What rendezvous?"

"The second rendezvous that we made. That was how the trouble began, and that's the whole story, messieurs."

Richardson pushed a written question over to Bigot. "Please ask her what she knows of a man named Novikoff, *alias* Polowski."

The question was put.

"Novikoff? I know no one of that name, and this time, messieurs, I assure you I *am* telling the truth."

At a sign from Bigot Verneuil left the room and two minutes later marshalled Polowski to the open door.

"Look, madame," said Bigot in a friendly tone. "Have you never seen this gentleman before?"

The woman looked round and broke into a laugh. "Ah! It's you, monsieur, that they are asking about. Of course I know that gentleman—only one does not waste time by asking gentlemen their names."

"Bring him in," said Bigot to Verneuil. "Now, madame, tell us how you met this man."

"There's very little to tell, monsieur. I was at the Café Weber one evening, not feeling at all well, and this gentleman and his friend put me into a taxi and took me safely home."

"Was it the evening when you met Marthe Lacour?"

"No, monsieur, it was the evening of the day when I did that little service for M. Pinet."

Bigot whispered to his subordinate, "You had better take her into the waiting-room and let her rest for a little, while I question this man."

"Come, madame," said Verneuil.

"Can I go home, then?"

Verneuil laughed sardonically. "Always thinking of going home, aren't you? No, you can't go home yet a while, but the sooner you come with me, the sooner we shall let you go."

"*Mon Dieu!*" exclaimed the woman, rising. "When one tells them the whole truth they will not let you go." She followed Verneuil wearily towards the waiting-room.

"Now, monsieur," exclaimed Bigot. "We should like to hear from you what happened on the night when you escorted that woman home."

Chapter Twenty-Two

"NOW, MONSIEUR, you are a foreigner. What is your nationality?"

"I am a Pole, born at Warsaw forty-three years ago. My name is Polowski."

"Your first name?"

"Ivan."

"But when you registered at your hotel you gave the name of Ivan Novikoff."

"Ah! Yes, that is my professional name."

"It is an offence, nevertheless. Show me your passport."

"Your officers have taken all my papers away to examine; my passport was among them."

"I'll look at your papers later. Carry on. When did you arrive in Paris?"

"About five weeks ago."

"What business are you doing in Paris?"

"I am a travelling jeweller. I am here on business."

"Selling jewellery, do you mean?"

"Yes, jewellery and precious metals. Perhaps you will allow me to put a question to you. A police officer stopped me and my friend in the street and brought us here as if we were criminals. That is not in accordance with traditional French hospitality to foreigners. I ask you why we were brought here."

Bigot waved the question aside. "The point is, monsieur, how you came to know that woman who has just gone out."

"What she told you just now was true."

"I want to hear the story in your own words."

"Well, it is soon told. We went to the café rather late in the evening, my friend and I. That woman was having an argument with the waiter as we came out; she was the only person sitting in the chairs on the street. As we passed the waiter stopped us and said in a low voice that the woman had drunk more than was good for her and was displaying a big roll of notes; he did not think that it was safe for her to go home alone. The woman overheard him and said, 'I am all right; there's nothing the matter with me. If these gentlemen will call a taxi I'll get into it and go straight home.' A taxi was passing at the moment, and my friend hailed it. I asked her for her address to give to the driver; she pushed the door open and invited us into the taxi, saying, 'If you don't come, I may fall out, and then how will you feel?' People were collecting to listen, and so we jumped in, and she gave her address."

"Did you try to sell her any jewellery on the way?"

"No, I did not. I asked her if it was true that she had a big roll of notes on her, and she pulled out of her handbag a thick wad of notes. I told her to put them away quick; that if anyone saw them at that late hour she might get robbed."

"Did she tell you where she got the notes?"

"I asked her that. She said that they were given to her by a friend for what she had done for him, and after a little pressing she told us the name of the friend, a M. Pinet, a French journalist who lived in a house in le Pecq. I don't know why you are asking me all these questions. If it is that you think that we received any money from the woman, you are quite mistaken. She was quite equal to guarding her fortune literally by tooth and nail. When we put her down at her own door she did not even offer to pay for the taxi; she went off leaving us to pay her fare."

"And having got this information that M. Pinet had won the first prize in the lottery, you called on him at his house in le Pecq?"

"Yes—on a matter of business."

"Did you know the names of any other winners of big prizes?"

"No, I did not know the names of any other winners."

Richardson had handed up another question. Had he heard that a Mr. Everett, an attaché to the British Embassy, had won a prize? The question was put. Novikoff shook his head and said that he had never heard of the gentleman.

"Where were you on October 6th?"

"On October 6th? I should have to look up my diary to answer that question."

"We can look it up in your diary, monsieur. We have it here."

"Oh! Then you have searched our rooms at the hotel? I see, but I should like to know on what ground you embarked on this strange proceeding."

Bigot made no reply to him. He turned to Verneuil. "Very good, brigadier, you can take the gentleman back to his companion and let him wait for the present."

When the witness had been removed Bigot turned to Richardson. "You may have guessed from my last questions to that man that I was trying to get an admission from him that he had been to M. Everett's flat on the evening of the murder. As you thought it possible that M. Everett might have been the winner of one of the other big prizes, I put inquiries, but as you saw, I drew blank. It may be true, indeed, that Polowski has never seen Everett."

"I ought to tell you, M. Bigot," said Richardson, "that in the desk used by Mr. Everett at the British Embassy I found a number in a notebook that might have been the number of a lottery ticket. The figures puzzled me at the time. Would it be possible for you, between now and to-morrow, to procure the winning numbers of all the big prizes?

"Oh, yes, monsieur, that can be done. And now I should like to ask you whether we shall charge the two men downstairs with attempted fraud in trying to sell gold to M. Cooper when he was posing as M. Rivaux from Canada?"

Richardson was horror-struck, though no one would have guessed it from his expression.

"Oh, no, monsieur. We don't want to bring Mr. Cooper forward as a witness."

"It's of no consequence, monsieur. We have that gold brick of theirs, found in their rooms, and that will be sufficient to support a charge of cheating."

"Before we separate," said Richardson, "would it not be well to look at that diary of his?"

"Certainly, *chère camarade*. Here it is."

Richardson fluttered through the leaves. "Here is the date—October 6th. Why, according to this entry the man was in Marseilles on October 6th and did not reach Paris until the 7th."

"If that entry is correct he is cleared of all complicity in the murder. And now, messieurs, I think you will agree that we've done enough for this evening. To-morrow I propose to bring in Pinet and that platinum blonde lady of his for interrogation. We may be able to formulate a charge against the woman of trying to poison Thérèse Volny."

"Yes, monsieur; and we must not forget to question her about the photographs she took at Vincennes, for those photographs were afterwards found undeveloped on the scene of the crime."

"True, but if I have those two brought down we shall also search their villa from top to bottom, and I shall be surprised if we do not find the camera that she used. Yes, we will have a field day with those two to-morrow."

The two English police officers took their leave, and as they were walking back to their hotel Richardson said, "I wonder whether we could catch Mr. Gregory at his flat now. I should like to have a word with him about those figures we found in the note-book. They may not have been those of a lottery ticket at all."

They were just in time; they met Ned Gregory coming down the stairs from his flat, attired in a dinner jacket. On seeing them he looked at his watch. "Anything urgent?" he asked.

"I only want five minutes, Mr. Gregory, but we mustn't make you late for your engagement."

"If it's only five minutes and I take a taxi instead of walking, all will be well. Come along; we'll run ourselves up in the lift."

Richardson wasted no time in putting his question. "You remember that I showed you a note-book we found in Mr. Everett's desk at the Embassy? The last entry was a set of figures. Do you think it possible that it was the number of a lottery ticket?"

"H'm! If it was a lottery ticket the thing was highly irregular. At the Embassy everybody is on his honour not to take tickets in any kind of lottery, because the Embassy is by way of being British soil, and lotteries are illegal in Great Britain. But I won't say that no member of the staff has ever been known to infringe this unwritten rule; indeed, I should be surprised if in a fit of absence of mind I had not broken the rule myself."

"Well, sir, we are taking steps to get the numbers of all the winners of big prizes in the last lottery. I hope to have them to-morrow morning."

"Do you mean that the number of a lottery ticket may become a clue?" asked Gregory incredulously.

"I mean, sir, that if Mr. Everett had been lucky and had drawn out a considerable sum of money from the lottery, it would supply the thing which has always been lacking in the case—a motive for the murder."

"I wish I could stop to thrash this out, inspector, but I shan't forget what you've said. Let me know as early as possible whether those figures in the notebook fit any of the winning tickets. And now I must be off."

When the two police officers were in the street together Cooper remarked, "I think we ought to celebrate to-night, inspector. Think of it. I've been a Canadian millionaire for four days, watching my step all the time, and to-night I'm back as plain Detective Sergeant Cooper. Let us do ourselves well, if only to make the transition a little more gradual."

"Very well; we'll walk along the Boulevard until we see a likely looking place for getting good cooking at a reasonable figure. You know, Cooper, we've had ups and downs in this case, and it is only this evening that I feel that we may be turning the corner."

"Turning the corner, you call it? Bless you, I know when you turned the corner. It was two days ago," responded Cooper. "But you're quite right. We won't discuss it until we're sure."

They dined at an establishment of Cooper's choice, not wisely nor too well, but Richardson could cheer-fully have lived on a convict diet that evening—the future had taken on a rose colour in the near horizon. They both slept soundly that night.

It was barely nine o'clock when they presented themselves at the police headquarters of the ninth *arrondissement*. Their two friends, Bigot and Verneuil, were already at work. They had before them the ticket numbers of the first twenty-one prizes—the first prize of five millions and the twenty prizes of one million each. Richardson had brought with him the little note-book in which the figures 070564/18 was the last entry. There was scarcely need to take seats around the table, for at the head of Bigot's list were the figures 070564Sie18.

"And that was the ticket presented by the woman Thérèse Volny when she drew the money," said Bigot.

"Yes," said Cooper, "and she drew that money for Pinet."

Richardson sat silent, thinking. "Before you bring M. Pinet down for examination, M. Bigot, could we not trace the person who sold this winning ticket?"

"That has already been done, monsieur. It was a tobacconist in the Place de la Madeleine."

"I know the place; it is next door to Cook's travel agency. I have bought cigarettes there," said Richardson. "If you will allow me, I should like to visit that shop with you or the Brigadier Verneuil at once. They may remember to whom they sold that winning ticket."

Bigot, being the senior of the two officers, elected to go with them to the tobacconist, while Verneuil, taking two officers with him, would go down to le Pecq to bring back the occupants of the Villa Mariette, and would search the premises for a camera or any other object of interest in the case.

Arrived in the Place de la Madeleine, Bigot led the way into the tobacconist's. In the shop they found the elderly manageress and two or three young assistants, who seemed to have been selected for their looks as well as their intelligence. There being other customers in the shop, Bigot drew the manageress aside and explained to her the nature of his visit. The lady beamed.

"Yes, monsieur, it was we who sold the winning ticket in the second *tranche*. One of my assistants, Mademoiselle Madeleine, will tell you about the purchaser. I will call her. Mademoiselle Madeleine!"

"Coming, madame." She was engaged at the moment with a customer. And then a young woman of vivacity and charm stood before them. "Ah!" she exclaimed, "I wondered when someone would come. You've brought my little present, monsieur?"

"Your present?"

"Yes. The English gentleman who bought from me the winning ticket promised me a present if he won. He said that I was to give the number my blessing and then he would be sure to win, and I, knowing that Englishmen never break their word, kept the number of his ticket always. Imagine, then, my astonishment and my delight when I saw that this was the number that had won the five million prize."

"Does mademoiselle remember the gentleman who bought it?"

"I remember him very well. He used to come here nearly every day, but he hasn't been for quite a long time now."

"He never told you his name, I suppose?"

"Oh, no, monsieur, but he was an Englishman. He spoke French fluently, but with an English accent that was unmistakable."

"Can you describe him?" asked Richardson.

"Yes, monsieur. I can see him now. He had fair hair and blue eyes, and a light moustache which was clipped short. He was about your own height and build."

"How much did the Englishman promise you if he won?" asked Bigot.

"He did not mention the exact sum, monsieur, but it was to be something substantial out of his winnings. Naturally, he did not count upon winning the first prize."

"Have no fear, mademoiselle; you can leave that matter in my hands. There will be quite a nice little sum in his present to you."

As the three officers walked back towards the station, Richardson said, "Have you a reward fund on which you can draw, monsieur?"

"A reward fund? I do not understand."

"You led that young lady to expect a substantial reward out of the Englishman's winnings."

"Ah! Now I understand. No, it is not the police who will pay the reward; that will come from the money we find in M. Pinet's house when we search it, for you see what has happened. We don't know the whole story as yet, but if M. Pinet and the Englishman shared this ticket between them and Pinet has chosen to collect the whole sum, he cannot complain if we take some of it to pay what was promised to that young lady."

"I confess that I do not yet understand the system on which the lottery is drawn," said Richardson.

"The lottery is drawn in public and the newspapers are free to publish the winning numbers."

"And the names and addresses of the winners?"

"Ah, no. If that were done many people would refrain from buying tickets. Think, monsieur, what would happen to them if their names and addresses were published. There would be an unending procession to their houses. Every business firm that sold yachts and motor-cars and wireless apparatus and ingenious toys for washing dishes and making ice and sweeping floors would send travellers to give demonstrations; every impecunious man who had failed in every attempt to make a living would call to ask for some of the money. The postman would collapse under the weight of letters he would have to carry every morning. No; whatever else is published it must not be the name or address."

"But I remember paragraphs about winners in the lottery."

"Yes, monsieur, but those paragraphs were communicated by foolish persons who took pride in winning and did not guess at the punishment they were bringing on themselves."

"Then you mean that if I buy a ticket which wins the first prize, there is no official record of my name as the purchaser as there is in lotteries in some other countries."

"That is so, monsieur."

"And if the ticket is stolen from me I have no redress?"

Bigot laughed. "You must not let it be stolen from you, monsieur, since whoever brings your ticket to the Pavilion Flore will receive the money."

Chapter Twenty-Three

THEY TURNED into the police station; an orderly came forward with a telephone message. "From Brigadier Verneuil," he said.

Bigot read it and handed it to Richardson. It ran:

"Have arrested the two persons. Coming by next train; premises searched; missing camera found."

"Now, messieurs, we have to make our plans. Pinet and his woman should be here in an hour; it is now close upon eleven. I propose that we break off now until a quarter to one before we begin the interrogation."

"And let the prisoners have their *déjeuner*?" inquired Richardson.

Bigot waved a derisive forefinger before his face. "If you want a prisoner to make confidences, never fill his stomach before you begin. His memory is more active on an empty stomach; it is a golden rule."

Richardson made no comment upon this cynical remark. He and Cooper turned to go, saying that they would come back at a quarter to one.

"If you'd been in his place," said Cooper, "you wouldn't have broken off the inquiry just at this point."

"I should not, but since the interrogation of prisoners is not allowed with us it is difficult to criticize the system."

"I wonder whether these interrogations, as they call them, help the police in getting at the truth?"

"Occasionally, as in this case, they may, but on the whole I wouldn't exchange the French system for ours," replied Richardson. "Now this may prove to be your last luncheon in Paris."

"Our last *déjeuner*? Aren't you a bit over-sanguine?"

"I feel that we are on the verge of clearing up the case. Where shall we go?"

"What about trying one of those snack lunches they advertise at the Café Weber? They seem to serve them at any hour."

"Very well, but I can't pretend to have an appetite at 11.30 a.m. I'll do my best. It's a good way of killing time."

They contrived to kill time so very agreeably that they were surprised when they found that they were due to start for the police station.

Verneuil met them as they came in and followed them into the big room. His eyes were twinkling with satisfaction. He shut the door behind them with care and then proceeded to unfold his tale.

"You have the two prisoners here?" asked Richardson.

The other nodded, pointing downward towards the cells.

"Have they told you anything since you arrested them?"

"They've been too busy quarrelling between themselves for me to do anything but listen. And look you! They are frightened, and fear is apt to loose the tongue. Each blames the other."

"You found the camera that fitted those films?"

"I found more than that. I found a coat stiff with dried blood. I showed it to the gentleman, saying, 'Whose blood is that?' He turned as white as that sheet of paper and said, 'I got that injury when I fell off my motor-bicycle in the Place de la Concorde.' 'Oh!' said I, 'you told us then that your nose had bled, but never have I seen nose-bleeding as profuse as this must have been. This coat must be shown to the surgeons; they will be able to say whether the blood came from the nose.' That depressed him, I can tell you, for the blood is all over the front of the coat. He is now in a very promising state for blurting out the truth."

"And the woman?" inquired Richardson.

"Oh! She is a very different proposition. She will talk—yes— but if she came within speaking distance of the truth you would never get it. It is the man we must tackle while he's frightened."

"The two are not together?"

"No; they won't see one another until Pinet has coughed up the truth."

"When are you going to interrogate them?"

"Ah! That decision rests with the Great Chief," replied Verneuil with a wry smile. "I will go and tell him that the two have arrived, and that you also are waiting upon his pleasure."

He stumped out of the room and returned almost immediately with Bigot, who seemed pathetically anxious to create an impression upon his British colleagues, and gave them seats of honour on either side of him. Pinet was sent for.

Verneuil's demeanour to his captive did not err on the side of gentleness. He held the man by his arm and shook him as he forced him to take the chair opposite to Bigot. Richardson expected a protest, but none came. The man was cowed; he cast a furtive glance at the two British officers and seemed to commend his protection to Providence.

"Your name?" rapped out Bigot.

"Henri Pinet."

"You are a journalist?"

"Yes; I write for the *Crédit National.*"

"In that capacity you knew M. Everett, the Press attaché to the British Embassy in Paris?"

"Yes."

"And you visited him in his apartment on the evening of his death. Why?"

"I went to ask him for some information on British finance for my paper."

"While you were there you dropped an un-developed film containing pictures of animals at Vincennes."

"No, monsieur."

"Now, come. I warned you to tell the truth, and now you tell the same falsehood as you did when you were questioned at your house in le Pecq. How can you say no when a camera which the film fits has been found in your house, and the film was exposed by a lady who was living with you at le Pecq, and you were with her when she exposed it? You see, we know a good deal more about your movements and hers than you think we do."

"I had forgotten it, monsieur," stammered Pinet.

Bigot laughed cynically. "Tell me this: you, like other Parisian journalists, were present at the drawing of the second *tranche* of the National Lottery. Is that not so?"

Richardson saw the man cower in his chair. He nodded.

"You and the dead man were sharing a ticket between you?"

"No, monsieur, you are wrong. Each of us had a whole ticket."

"Then tell me this. M. Everett had the ticket that won five millions. You were present when that ticket was drawn."

"I did not take note of the number."

"No? And yet you were present as the representative of a financial paper?"

"Well, I may have heard the number, but it has since escaped me."

Bigot thumped the oak table with his clenched fist. "Understand, monsieur, this is not the moment for telling imaginative stories. You are here to give true answers to my questions. Was not the winning ticket number 070564 series 18?"

"I believe that it was, monsieur."

"And that was the ticket held by the dead man. How, then, do you account for having sent the woman Thérèse Volny to the Pavilion Flore with that ticket to collect the money and pay it over to you? How do you explain that?"

The man in the chair swallowed painfully, but made no reply.

"She did not know M. Everett; therefore, she must have got the ticket from you, and that means that you murdered him and stole it from him."

Pinet had turned very white and his lips were dry; he moistened them with his tongue. "I didn't murder him; I defended myself. He attacked me first."

"Why should he attack you?"

"Because I was looking at his ticket, and I suppose he thought..."

"...That you were stealing it?"

The young man began to catch his breath as if he were about to sob. "I'll tell you the whole truth, monsieur. I called on M. Everett that night, partly on business, as I told you. I said to him that I had been present at the draw and had noted the numbers of all the big prizes. He went to a drawer and took out his lottery ticket and laid it on the table, and then, with true British phlegm, instead of immediately examining the numbers, he said, 'We must have a drink to give us strength for the shock of not winning.' He turned to the buffet, which has a mirror behind it. I did not notice the mirror, and on a sudden temptation I tried to substitute my ticket for his, which bore the winning number. Then he attacked me; tried to drag my papers out of my pocket. He was stronger than I was; I felt my strength oozing away and his fingers feeling for my throat. I snatched up a dagger, meaning only to threaten him with it, but he caught at my wrist and I struck at him with it. There was a rush of blood which stained my clothing. He fell on the floor and I left him, slamming the door behind me. That is the whole story. If he had not attacked me he would be alive to-day. Anyone in my place would have done the same."

At a sign from Bigot, Verneuil took the rough notes of the statement out with him to the typist and signed to Pinet to follow him. "When we've got this typed out you will sign it," he said.

Fortunately Cooper also had made a copy of the statement, and the two British officers half rose from their seats. An abrupt leave-taking was far less than M. Bigot thought that he had a right to expect.

"*Eh bien!*" he said, "you gentlemen have seen how we conduct our business in France. If an interrogation be properly handled, a full confession is the result. You have seen this for yourselves."

"Indeed, monsieur, it was a remarkable success for the police," said the diplomatic Richardson. They parted cordially.

"You will leave the case in our hands, knowing that justice will be done?" were Bigot's parting words.

Safe out in the street Richardson breathed a sigh of relief. "I am glad to have seen for myself how the French system works, and I'm glad that interrogations are not allowed in England."

"The system suits these people all right," remarked Cooper, "but that self-satisfied Bigot would never have got Pinet to cough up if he hadn't had the evidence we collected for him up his sleeve. Where are we going now?"

"First to the Embassy to make our verbal report; then to our hotel to pack up. We'll catch to-night's boat train."

At the Embassy they found that Gregory was in his room. To him they recounted Pinet's confession.

"You mean to say that they got all that out of him without using the thumbscrew?"

"There seemed to be threats looming in the back-ground. They assured us that justice would be done."

Gregory permitted himself to laugh. "You know, of course, what will happen? The *procureur* de la République will formulate a charge of murder; Pinet's counsel will draw tears from the jury by representing his client as the victim of a brutal Englishman who would have killed him had he not defended himself. The jury will give a verdict of justifiable homicide without leaving the box. Pinet will be set free to enjoy the remainder of the five millions and become a deputy."

"I don't think that he will get a very large share of the five millions, sir—not if I know the Brigadier Verneuil, who did the searching."

"Well, they must settle it among themselves. We can't claim any of it for poor Everett's heirs, because technically he had no business as a British subject to take part in a lottery. Do you think that the confession was a true one?"

"Yes, sir, I do," said Richardson. "When I first visited Mr. Everett's flat and found a glass half full of whisky and an uncorked bottle, I happened to stoop, and in the mirror behind the buffet I saw the entire room. It occurred to me then that the visitor, whoever he was, had been caught in the act of robbing his host."

"You'll let us have a report for the ambassador before you go?"

"Not before we leave, sir. We propose to cross by the night boat, but the ambassador shall have a copy of our full report to-morrow from London."

"You take my breath away. Surely you're going to say good-bye to us here."

Richardson looked at his watch. "If any of your colleagues would like to see us, sir, but probably they are all busy at this hour."

"Sit tight and I'll see." Gregory left the room at a run and came back to say that the first secretary, Mr. Eric Carruthers, would like to see them. He conducted them along the passage to Carruthers' room and ushered them in. "They want to catch to-night's boat," he said.

"We can't let you go, Mr. Richardson, until you've seen the ambassador; it won't take five minutes. Come along; I'll take you upstairs."

They found Sir Wilfred Bryant in his pleasant room, overlooking the Embassy garden.

"The police officers from Scotland Yard, sir," announced Carruthers. "They propose to leave to-night."

The ambassador swung round in his chair. "You've had to give the case up?" he asked querulously.

"No, sir," replied Carruthers; "they've cleared the case up and they've got a confession from the murderer."

The ambassador stared at him incredulously. "Got a confession after barely a week's work?"

"Ten days, sir," corrected Richardson, a stickler for accuracy.

"Well, ten days. Thank heaven I sent for you. When am I to have your report?"

"It will go to the Foreign Office to-morrow, Your Excellency. I am afraid that I have no copy to leave with you, because it is not yet written."

"What would happen to us all if we worked at such high pressure?" murmured the ambassador under his breath. "I'm very much obliged to you, and if you are really going to-night I mustn't detain you longer."

When the two detective officers had bowed themselves out the ambassador said, "Now, perhaps, you'll admit that we did right in sending for those men. But for them and their energy, think what would have happened. Those ghastly newspapers would have worked the case up into a political assassination, whereas it was in reality nothing but a squalid crime of robbery and murder."

THE END

www.ingramcontent.com/pod-product-compliance
Lightning Source LLC
Chambersburg PA
CBHW070311190726
48291CB00012B/1075